PRAISE FOR

The Sweet Everlasting

"A story told in language as plain as an old quilt . . . with a tenderness and depth of feeling that will haunt you long after the reading."
—*Atlanta Journal-Constitution*

"A novel that plumbs the depths of human suffering and celebrates the courage and dignity that enable its hero to endure . . . Mitcham manipulates his narrative with a masterful hand, leading us, in the end, to a series of revelations as startling as they are apt. *The Sweet Everlasting* is a dark but lyrical novel that probes the human condition so closely that it hurts." —*Richmond Times-Dispatch*

"Moving and well-written." —*Los Angeles Times*

"Deeply affecting . . . a haunting story beautifully told." —*Publishers Weekly* (starred review)

"Scene after scene of stunning precision and clarity. The straight and simple voice of this novel can break your heart." —*Boston Globe*

Sabbath Creek

Sabbath Creek

A NOVEL BY

Judson Mitcham

The University of Georgia Press

ATHENS AND LONDON

Published by the University of Georgia Press
Athens, Georgia 30602
© 2004 by Judson Mitcham
All rights reserved
Designed by Sandra Strother Hudson
Photograph by Douglas K. Hill
Set in Adobe Garamond
Printed and bound by Maple-Vail
The paper in this book meets the guidelines for permanence
and durability of the Committee on Production Guidelines
for Book Longevity of the Council on Library Resources.

Printed in the United States of America
04 05 06 07 08 C 5 4 3 2 1

Library of Congress Cataloging-in-Publication Data
Mitcham, Judson.
Sabbath Creek : a novel / by Judson Mitcham.
p.   cm.
ISBN 0-8203-2577-5 (alk. paper)
1. Boys—Fiction. 2. Georgia—Fiction. 3. Poor families—Fiction.
4. Fathers—Death—Fiction. 5. Mothers and sons—Fiction. I. Title.
PS3563.I7356 S23 2004
813'.54—dc22   2003015704

British Library Cataloging-in-Publication Data available

Excerpt from "A Journal of the Year of the Ox" from *The World of the
Ten Thousand Things: Poems 1980–1990* by Charles Wright. Copyright
© 1990 by Charles Wright. Reprinted by permission of Farrar, Straus
and Giroux, LLC. Excerpt from "Island" from *The Collected Poems of
Langston Hughes* by Langston Hughes. Courtesy of A. A. Knopf.

FOR JEAN, ZACH, AND ANNA

How shall we hold on, when everything bright falls away?
How shall we know what calls us
                              when what's past remains what's past
And unredeemed, the crystal
And wavering coefficient of what's ahead?

CHARLES WRIGHT

Wave of sorrow,
Do not drown me now.

LANGSTON HUGHES

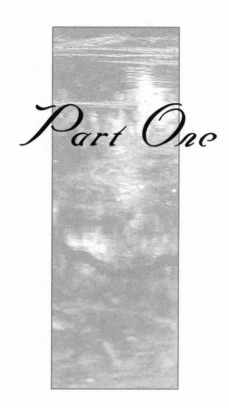

Part One

1

He slammed down the hood, then elbowed me out of the way, trailing an odor of old sweat and cigars and loud cologne soured in his clothes. He told my mother he would order the part, but it might not arrive for a week or even longer. She asked him if Sabbath Creek had a place where we could stay.

"Not really." He squinted at her and scratched under his arm and leaned closer. "There *is* this place down the road, maybe a mile out of town, old nigger place, but you and your boy don't want to stay there."

My mother took a deep breath as if to speak, but she did not. We pulled our bags out of the trunk and climbed into the cab of the tow truck—a tight fit since the man weighed maybe three hundred pounds, and I was big for my age. At nearly fourteen, I was almost the same size I am now, ten years later. My mother sat crushed against the door; she locked it, and she pulled back on the handle as we rode.

The Sabbath Creek Motor Court resembled a chickenhouse reconceived as a motel—a long low strip of rooms, most of the windows broken out, the roof charred at the far end, wires sticking up like frizzy hair, no cars parked outside.

The man drove away, leaving us standing at the door where OFFICE had fallen off and left the outline of the letters. My mother pushed the doorbell button, waited, pushed it again.

She knocked on the door, and it swung open; she pulled it shut, then knocked again, louder, and she opened the door and shouted hello.

She stepped inside, and I followed her. The dim room, lit only by a small floor lamp, smelled damp and poisonous. There was a closed door on the other side of the counter, and she walked around and knocked again.

"Hey!" she yelled. "You've got customers."

I sat on the sofa, which enveloped me in its broken springs and moldy stink, and after a few more tries my mother came over, and the ruined couch swallowed her as well, and we waited there.

* * *

We heard a door thump shut, then the sound of a car driving off, and a moment later an old man came through the door, a tall, thin, dark-skinned black man wearing a baseball cap, tennis shoes, brown work pants, and a white shirt buttoned at the collar. The little bit of hair showing under his cap was as white as the shirt.

"Uh oh," he said when he saw us. "Y'all work for the sheriff?"

He performed a jerky little shuffle-step as he crossed the room to the counter, where he set down a large brown paper bag.

"No, sir," my mother said. "We . . ."

"Do I have the right to remain silent?"

"Well, no. You see, our car broke down . . ."

"*No?*" the man said. "You mean I got to keep talking? Can anything I say be used against me?"

"Look," she said, "we just need a room. Is that possible?"

"Say you need a *room?* All right then, all right. That's good. We got you a room."

My mother explained that we might need it for a few days, since our car had broken down and was being repaired.

"Re*paired?* Where at?"

"A place back in town," she said. "What was the name? Coleman's?"

"*Cole*man's? Coleman can't fix nothing. What you take it to Coleman for? I could've told you where to take it."

She asked him again if he had a room for us.

The old man looked down and shook his head. "*Cole*man's. Last time I left a car over at Coleman's, Richard M. Nixon was the president. I'd have my car towed up to Fitzgerald now — have it towed anywhere — before I let those boys at Coleman's work on it. You might *never* get that car back."

"Well, from the way you're talking," my mother said, "we might be moving in here for quite a while. So maybe you can give us a discount."

"Hold on now," he said. "You can't *move in.* Didn't nobody ask you to *move in,* did they?" He waited, and we just stood there, and then he said, "So what kind of room y'all want? We only got one kind. Matter of fact, right now, we only got one room fit to live in. Got to fix the toilets in the other ones. And it's cash only."

My mother said that was fine, and he handed her a card to fill out. When she was done, he picked it up and read aloud.

"Charlene and Lewis Pope, 1991 Hunt Road, Cofield, Georgia. This your real name?"

She took the card back, scratched out Pope, and wrote in Smith, her maiden name. The old man looked at it and scowled and puffed out his lips.

"Another one of them Smiths, huh? All right then," he said, "if that's what you want to go with. But at some point I may need to see some ID, Miss *Smith*."

She started to pull out her wallet, but he said, "Let it go for now. We'll just let it go. But if y'all start getting rowdy, you see, I might need to check it. See if you really who you say you are."

He put away the card and tossed a key onto the counter. It slid across and almost fell, but my mother caught it.

"Just go out the door here and take a left. First room you come to," he said. "You want a key too, son?"

"Yes, sir. I guess so."

"Well, that's too bad," he said. "We ain't got but one. Y'all will just have to make do. Room One. Go out the door here, take a *what?* Left. Next door you come to. Already open. I'll have to get you some sheets and pillowcases and soap and towels and so on. I'll get you a shower curtain, and I'll turn those mattresses over. You'll need some lightbulbs — they all burnt out. Have to get y'all some coat hangers. The TV does work, but you only get two stations, and they go in and out. I had me a satellite dish, but some white boys stole it. I'll have to plug in the air conditioner. You got to fix that plug in the socket just right. The fan might make some noise, but it'll cool you off. No telephone in there, but the toilet works, I know that. I use it myself, every morning. I hope that won't bother anybody. I'll be in and out in no time, and y'all will still be asleep, most likely. I get out earlier than most folks. I like to watch the sun come up."

My mother said, "So you'll be coming into our room in the morning?"

"I'm afraid so. My place back here," — he jerked his thumb toward the door behind him — "ain't had a working commode in twenty years. I had to give up on it. So I use Room One. I'll let myself in and out."

"All right then." My mother's voice had gone a little thin. She picked up another registration card. "It says here the manager is Truman Stroud. Is that you?"

"That's the name my mama gave me. I go by Stroud. The only one that ever called me Truman was my first wife, and I can't hardly remember her. You married?"

He asked *me* the question, not my mother.

"Not yet, Mr. Stroud."

"Stroud, son. Not mister nothing. Stroud. One word. When you *do* get married, before you do, you check with me, I'll tell you all about what to look for in a woman. I'm ninety-three years old, been married four times, and outlived every one. But they was all happy, and so was I. You don't see that a lot these days, do you?" He leaned over the counter toward my mother. "Fine-looking woman like yourself," he said, "got to be a husband somewhere. New or old."

"Mr. Stroud," she said.

"Does either of y'all understand plain American? Not mister nothing. Call me Stroud. That's all I answer to."

"Okay, then," she said. "Stroud. I don't believe my marriage is any of your business, is it?"

"Not none of *my* business at all. No, it's not, no ma'am. I see your point." He looked straight at me. "How about you, boy? You got a daddy?"

My mother snatched the key off the counter, turned, and picked up her bags. "That'll be enough, Mr. Stroud. And another thing. You'll have to find yourself another bathroom. We'll be paying for this one, and we'll be reserving it for our use only."

The old man made a big show of tipping his cap as we headed out the door. "So very *pleased* to have you with us."

2

We put our bags in the room, then walked down the road, hoping to find someplace to eat. We passed two mobile homes, a house the color of a school bus, a long driveway that curved back into the woods. After maybe half a mile we came to a store with a portable sign that read FURLOW'S COKE TWO 4 ONE LOTTERY. There were two gas pumps out front, both with plastic bags over the handles, and there were cars and trucks parked everywhere, but we went inside and found only a girl working the register and a boy who seemed to be her boyfriend, from the way they whispered back and forth, the way he leaned over the counter and touched her.

The girl said, "Welcome to Furlow's, y'all." She had short brown hair, and bright red splotches spotted her face and neck.

The boy pulled back and turned away, started to examine the rows of candy bars next to the counter.

My mother spoke to the girl, then pointed to a sign offering different kinds of biscuit sandwiches, as well as barbecue or hot wings.

"Pick out what you want for supper," she told me. "I think I'd better get a few things for the room."

I walked down the first aisle, then came back to the counter, where I saw a bowl filled with wooden animal figures—dogs and cows, but mostly fish. A hand-lettered sign taped to the bowl read "Good Luck Charms." I picked up a fish no more than an inch long.

"There's a retarded man that lives down on the creek that makes them," the girl said. "Carves them with his pocketknife. He brings them up here, and we sell them for him. He don't make but fifty cent on each one."

I pulled out two quarters and handed them toward the girl.

"No, it's two-fifty," she said. "But *he* don't make but fifty cent. It ain't fair, I know. I told Mr. Furlow, but he don't care. And the man that carves them, he can't talk or understand what you say to him either one, so he takes what you give him. It's a pity. He's a real nice man. He wouldn't hurt a soul, I don't believe, but it scares the devil out of you to look at him. His face is all burned and scarred up, and one of his eyes is missing, and the first time he come in here, I run into the back of the store, but Mr. Furlow made me come out front again, and then he told me all about him. He seems like a sweet man, just scary."

My mother set a can of bug spray, a can of Lysol, a roll of paper towels, and a screwdriver onto the counter. I asked her what the screwdriver was for.

"We'll see," she said.

The girl started ringing up our purchases and bagging them. She handed me the carving.

"Here you go," she said in a soft voice. "I hope that brings you some really good luck."

I never believed the little fish had anything to do with luck, but I did start to carry it with me all the time.

The boyfriend swung around. "What stinks?" he said. He picked up a pack of rolling papers and slung them onto the counter, then slid in front of me, pushing me back. "I was here first."

"Ronnie," the girl said.

"Ronnie what?"

The girl didn't answer, and the boyfriend said, "Ronnie let the dipshit go first? Ronnie get lost? Ronnie what?" He kicked backwards and his bootheel caught me on the shin, and I yelled and tried to grab him, but my mother stepped between us.

"How about this?" she said, the screwdriver in her hand snagged on his T-shirt and angled toward his throat. "Ronnie behave yourself, or you'll have trouble you can't even imagine. How about that?" She pulled him sideways, and he fell into a rack of potato chips and pork skins.

"Oh, I'm worried," the boy said. "I'm shaking now."

My mother said, "Do you know who I am?"

He stood still and glared at her, then looked over at me.

"You don't know who I am, do you?"

The boy cut his eyes toward the girl.

"I suggest you find out," my mother said.

He looked down at the floor and snickered, then walked to the door, where he turned and pointed at me. "I get you by yourself, I'll kick your ass, mama's boy." He went out, climbed into a red Ford pickup with oversized tires, and drove off fast.

The girl apologized and rang up the rest of our items. "He's just that way," she said. "He's real jealous. Twenty-one dollars and sixteen cent."

My mother smiled. I hated for people to leave the letter *s* off *cents,* and she knew that. We'd heard it a lot in the weeks since we'd left home and started driving all over south Georgia.

"He can be real sweet, though," the girl said. "Look at what he gave me." She held out her left hand. "He just gave it to me last Friday."

"Is that an engagement ring?"

"Yes, ma'am."

They planned to get married as soon as she graduated from high school, the girl said, in a year. She was pretty sure she'd be manager of the store by then.

"Ronnie didn't finish school, but he's got a job up in Fitzgerald. He works construction and makes real good money. Him and his brother went in and bought a place right up the road, and that's where we plan to live. I've been doing a little decorating on it, but there's not really much to do. It came with the furniture already in it."

My mother congratulated her, and we were almost out the door when she turned and walked back to the counter.

"You have any matches?"

The girl pointed to a tray holding a pile of matchbooks. "Those are free. Help yourself."

My mother picked up a couple of matchbooks. "It's none of my business," she said, "but is this what you plan on doing for the rest of your life? It's honest work, I know that, but ten years from now, do you think you'll still want to be living with Ronnie and working here?"

"Oh, no ma'am," the girl said. "I'm going to quit work, and we're going to have a big family. Ronnie says he don't like kids, but he don't really mean it. I know him better than that. Once he has some of his own, he'll like them."

My mother told the girl she hoped they'd be very happy together. She said thanks, and then, as my mother walked away from her, "By the way, ma'am, what you said to Ronnie? When you asked him did he know who you are? Well, can I ask you, who *are* you?" But my mother went on out the door.

3

I was playing baseball at Andy Wilbur's house one day when his older sister asked me if I knew that my mother looked like Natalie Wood.

"I guess so," I said, "maybe." I didn't know who Natalie Wood was or what she looked like, but I didn't want to admit that to Andy's sister. Not long afterwards, I saw the actress in an old movie, and I noticed the resemblance, but my mother's face was rounder, her nose sharper and a bit too long for Hollywood. It was the eyes, mostly — those dark eyes impossible to ignore, with pupils that always seemed wide and inviting, even when she was tired or angry or sad.

Once, when I was twelve, my parents and I went to the Atlanta airport to pick up Uncle Lewis. My mother had gone into the restroom, and my father and I were sitting at the gate, waiting and watching hundreds of people rush past. We sat there not talking for a while, and then my father waved his hand toward the moving crowds.

"People from all over the world," he said. "Tell me if you see a woman better looking than your mother."

I did look at the other women, but I didn't want to be comparing them with my mother, since the shapes and faces of women had begun to fill me with wild thoughts that I could barely control. My mother came out of the restroom, but I didn't really look at her.

I realize now that when I did look at her, I didn't see her; I had never really seen her. Even when I looked at her and concentrated, I didn't see her. And even when she spoke simply and clearly and only to me, and I listened to her, I didn't really hear her, either. All my life, I realize now, she had been a kind of absence, until the summer we left home and stayed at the Sabbath Creek Motor Court and everything happened, and then — in the middle of a thunderstorm, late one night when it was almost all over — there she was.

4

We found clean sheets on the beds, soap and towels in the bathroom, which had been scrubbed and smelled much better. The air conditioner gave out a low growl, but it did cool the room. There was a new deadbolt on the door. After we ate, there was nothing to do. I tried the TV, but the reception was fuzzy, the speaker buzzed, and the picture rolled.

I looked through my dictionary for a while, and then I felt it come over me again—that little shift, that falling away. It had started happening more and more. There was something wrong with me, I knew that. Maybe a brain disease. Maybe I was crazy. Words on the page made it happen—froze me, left me angry and nauseated and sad, as if I were being mocked, as if the words were mocking me.

A few weeks ago, I had seen a story on TV about a man who made himself whistle a tune and walk backwards every time he saw a cat, and now I was afraid of becoming like that man, whose life was so far out of his control.

Like that man, I had found ways to deal with my condition, those little episodes that words gave me. I could make them stop by slamming the book shut or throwing it. Or I could imagine the impossible—history without time, or a falling leaf understanding God, or understanding itself.

I slammed the dictionary shut and went out to look for a wall to throw a baseball against. I had seen nothing suitable on our walk to the store, so I went in the other direction, ran maybe a mile down the highway, but found nothing there either.

When I came back to the motel, I walked around to the back and discovered junk and trash everywhere, with barely any place to step, though a narrow path ran through the pile. I saw bags of garbage but also old clothes, pieces of broken furniture, mattresses and bed frames. I followed the path and walked out into the other half of the motel's backyard, which was neatly kept, the grass mowed not too long ago.

I saw where our room was—I recognized the new curtains—but the place behind the office, where Stroud lived, surprised me. It was much bigger than I'd imagined, extending back into the yard, with several extra rooms. On the far side were tall, bushy trees that hid his apartment from the road, and there was a gravel driveway cutting through those trees. I walked up close and tried to get a look inside the apartment. I couldn't see anything, but I knew somebody was in there—I heard a toilet flush.

The back door opened onto a patio that included a table, two lawn chairs, and one large wooden chair with a tall back and wide, flat arms. And there was a little statue, too—a lawn jockey about three feet tall, with a shiny black face, thick red lips, and white teeth set in a wild grin. We'd seen one of those near Hawkinsville the week before. My mother had pointed it out.

I walked on up the road, but I didn't find a good wall to throw against, so I returned the way I came, through the piles of trash, where I found a green baseball cap that was greasy and stiff and crusted with dirt. I liked the big S on the front, so I took it inside, filled the sink with hot water, dumped in some shampoo, and left the cap there to soak.

* * *

The next morning when we left the room, my mother locked our door, then stepped over to the motel office and knocked. This time, the door didn't swing open. She knocked again, then tried the knob, but it wouldn't turn.

"I thought we were going to eat," I said.

"We are, but I wanted to have a word with Mr. Stroud first."

"Stroud," I said.

She told me she planned to thank him for fixing up our room and to apologize for saying he couldn't use our toilet.

"I think he's got a bathroom," I said. "I think he was just having some fun with us."

I led her around to the far side of the motel, through the trees and up the gravel drive, and I showed her the apartment and told her I'd heard somebody flush a toilet in there last night.

I expected her to knock on the back door, but she didn't. "Let's go eat," she said, which was fine with me. I didn't want to knock at Stroud's private entrance; I was not sure he'd like it.

As we headed down the drive, I looked back and noticed that the lawn jockey's face was turned in our direction. There was an ashtray balanced on his head, and I thought I saw smoke rising from it.

5

I discovered an old house about a mile from the motel. Strips of fake brick siding curled up from the gray wood in spots. The windows were all broken out, the tin roof rusted a dark wine shade. I looked in and saw trash scattered around and a straight chair lying on its back.

I taped my strike zone to the side of the house, stepped off the distance, dug myself a pitching rubber with my heel, then threw for a long time, playing imaginary games and losing them, as usual, because I walked so many batters.

* * *

I followed the gravel driveway to Stroud's patio and found him sitting in the large wooden chair, his eyes closed, his arms resting on the chair's flat arms, his right hand around a glass, his left hand holding a cigarette with a long ash that had burned down almost to his fingers. I'd stopped walking and was standing still, maybe fifteen feet from the patio, when he turned and looked at me, his eyes bloodshot and watery yellow. He waved me over with his cigarette hand, ash flying through the air, and pointed to one of the lawn chairs.

"Have a seat." He swung his glass toward a small blue cooler. "Get you one of them sodas. Keep your hands off the Budweiser."

I pulled a Coke from the ice and popped it open and thanked him.

"You welcome, son."

We sat there sipping our drinks. Neither of us spoke, but he studied me so closely that I felt uneasy. I pretended to rub something off the back of my hand, inspected the side of the Coke can, pulled at my shoelaces, but when I glanced up again, he was still looking me over.

Finally, he said, "That's the way my folks taught me, you see. Somebody says thank you, you say they *what?* Welcome. Not 'uh huh,' like you hear folks say now. Or 'You bet.' I've heard folks say that. 'You bet.' I didn't bet nothing. Somebody says thank you, you say they *welcome.*"

I'd heard my father say something similar, and I told him that.

"So you do have a daddy then. Your mama got a husband. See now? What's the big secret?"

He pointed to a brown paper bag beside the cooler. "Reach in there, get you some of them boiled peanuts. They still hot. Salty, like I like them."

I pulled a few peanuts out of the bag, then held it out to the old man, who shook his head no. "I done ate too many already," he said. "They don't sit well with my stomach after while. Get you a handful."

I told him that my mother and I had stopped by his office to thank him for fixing up our room, but that he hadn't answered the door. He stubbed out his cigarette in the ashtray that sat on the lawn jockey's head.

"Tell your mama she's welcome."

"And she said you could use our bathroom."

"Did she now?" He gave out a wheezy chuckle. "Did she?" He stopped, a look of fake surprise on his face, and he seemed to be waiting for an answer.

"Yes, sir."

"Well," he said, speaking more slowly now, drawing out his words, "you tell your mama that's mighty white of her, son. Sho nuff is. Sho nuff. Reach in there and get you some more peanuts. Get all you want. And take some for your pretty mama too."

6

I woke up, and my mother was gone again. I walked all the way around the motel and saw that Stroud's lights were still on, though it was after three in the morning. All his curtains were open, and I could see him as clearly as though he were on stage.

He never sat down but moved from room to room, picking up things and looking at them. He stood in his kitchen, staring at the salt shaker in his hand, then put it back, walked to the next room, picked up a little wooden box and studied that for a while, then returned it to the shelf, stepped close to a lamp and ran his finger along the shade.

I left Stroud's yard as quietly as I could, headed toward Furlow's, and when I got there, I saw my mother hanging up the pay phone outside the store.

"You promised you wouldn't do this again," I said, and then I saw she'd been crying, and I asked her what was wrong.

"I called your father, that's all. I'm all right." She started back toward the motel, walking fast.

"Why'd you do that?"

"I've been doing it all along," she said, "just to see if he'll answer."

We were far from any lights, and there was no moon. We walked past a dead animal that was ripe in the heat. I'd passed it on the way to the store and planned to hold my breath when I came to it again, but it surprised me, and I inhaled the smell deeply before I knew I'd done it, and then I had the taste of a dead thing in my mouth.

* * *

I went for a long run, followed the road down into pine canyons where the night's cool still held on, then out past cleared land, the long sloping acres of green burning silver with dew. All I could hear was my own breath and footsteps, and after a while it felt like my legs were moving on their own. At the one-hour mark, I turned around and headed for the motel, and when I got there, I found a note from my mother.

Have gone out. Be here when I get back.

I took a shower, then lay on the bed and waited. Maybe she was calling my father again.

I heard what sounded like a gunshot, far off. About a minute later, I heard three more, rapid fire, and then it was quiet.

7

Stroud told me he needed some help, and he took me into his apartment. All the curtains were pulled back, and the whole place was bright with sun, and it smelled fresh, like lemon-scented furniture polish. I helped him lift a heavy box onto a shelf.

"All right then," he said. "I appreciate it. Hold it right there," — he pointed at my feet — "I got a little something for you." He went into the kitchen and came back with a single saltine. I thanked him and took the cracker and ate it.

The walls were covered with photographs, nearly all framed, most of them in black and white.

"Who are all these people?" I asked him.

"Who *are* they?" he shot back. "Who are *you?*"

He seemed to be waiting for me to answer, but I had no idea what to say — I hadn't intended to insult anybody — so I shrugged and said, "I don't know."

"Don't *know?* Ain't you Lewis Pope? Checked in here with your mama a few days ago? Ain't that you?"

"Yes, sir, I guess so."

"You better quit guessing," he said. "Say it straight out. Get some spine and stand up. You hear me?"

I nodded, but I was afraid to say anything.

He waved his hand toward the back door. "Step on out here with me while I have a cigarette." We went through the kitchen and onto the patio, and he took the large wooden chair and I sat in one of the others. He pulled a pack of cigarettes from his pocket and held it out to me, looking over the tops of his glasses. I reached out to take one—though I didn't plan to smoke it—and he pulled it back.

"Look here," he said. "First thing you got to learn is a little common sense. You follow me?"

"Yes, sir."

He shook a cigarette up from the pack, pulled it out with his lips, and lit it.

"Second thing," he said, "is this. You want to be a ballplayer, don't you ever get started on these things. They suck the wind right out of you. Give the other fellow a little edge, you see, and a little edge is all a good player will need."

I asked him how he knew I wanted to be a ballplayer.

He started laughing, and the laugh ratcheted into a cough, and he pulled a handkerchief from his pants pocket, put it to his mouth—I heard him clear his throat and spit—and then he folded the handkerchief and put it back in his pocket.

"How did I *know?* Look here, you ain't invisible. I believe sometimes white folks go around thinking they invisible. Here you are, running up and down the road with your ball glove, and you done gone out to the old Stiles place and pasted up a strike zone—a whole lot bigger than it ought to be—on the side of the house, and you out there throwing like it was the World Series, walking around talking to yourself, and you think can't nobody see you. Why you think that is?"

I started to tell him I didn't know, but I caught myself. Then I told him I didn't think it had anything to do with my being white.

He took out his handkerchief again and laughed and coughed and wheezed some more, but this time he looked like he was in pain, and I stood up and told him I thought maybe I should leave.

"Sit down." He choked out the words. "Go on, sit down."

He pointed at the cooler and said, "Get yourself one of them co-colas. Go on, it won't hurt you, long as that ain't what you live on. I knew this woman lived on co-cola and that was it. Didn't eat or drink nothing else. Backyard was full of bottles, them old-time co-cola bottles, little heavy green bottles. All she did, all day long, was drink them sodas. She had open-ers all over the walls. She'd spilled so much co-cola, the floors rotted through. Woman never left the house. When she died, they found barbed wire strung around the inside of the house, wire like they have on top of the fence over at the jail. And she knew she was dying, because she left a note saying somebody'd poisoned her. I wonder who *that* was?"

I popped open the can and took a swallow. "If she never left the house, how did she get the drinks?"

"Shoot. She had the truck come right to the house. One of the man's regular rounds, like she was a Piggly Wiggly all by herself. I seen him unloading the cases one time, and it took him a half hour."

"How did she pay for everything?"

"I didn't say the woman was poor, did I? Did I say she was poor?"

"No, sir."

"Well. But she *was,* though. Didn't have nothing. She got a check every month and signed it over to the co-cola man. That's what people said, anyhow. I don't know if it's true."

"Maybe she was crazy," I said.

"Think so?"

"I guess," I said. "Don't you?"

"Well," he said, "folks talk about crazy like they know what it is. I do know that for a fact. But she did love them sodas."

8

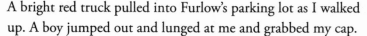

A bright red truck pulled into Furlow's parking lot as I walked up. A boy jumped out and lunged at me and grabbed my cap.

"Look who we got here," he said.

The cap was my favorite. Greg Maddux had signed his name on the underside of the bill when he'd visited a store in Macon earlier that summer. We'd driven there to see him, and I'd stood in line for over an hour.

The boy squirted a gob of spit on the cap, dropped it and stepped on it and ground it into the dirt. I ran at him hard, caught him in the stomach with the top of my head, locked my hands behind him and lifted, churned my legs and drove forward, and he slammed against the packed dirt, his back scraping against the rocks, and I could feel the top of my skull go into his gut and up against his ribcage when he hit the ground. He lay curled in on himself, rocking back and forth, trying to suck air. He was still holding the cap, but I took it away from him, then ran.

Back at the motel, I submerged the Braves cap in a sink full of hot soapy water—hoping the signature wouldn't wash off—and I put on the green cap with the big *S*. It was clean now—I'd dried it out in the sun, and it smelled pretty good, and I liked the way it looked on my head.

I ran past Coleman's Auto and saw our car up on blocks, with no tires, and I went inside. Only one man was working there. He wiped off his greasy hands with a rag, looked through some papers, then said our part was on back order, and he had no way to predict when it would arrive.

"Why did you take the tires off?" I asked him. "There was nothing wrong with the tires."

He screwed up his face. "Tires? Who said anything about tires?" He dropped the papers onto the desk and started wiping his hands again. "I got to get back to work now."

"Wait a minute," I said. "Our car's out there on blocks. What happened to the tires?"

"Look, you little piss ant. You got a complaint, take it up with Mr. Coleman. I just work here is all."

"Okay, then," I said. "Where's Mr. Coleman?"

"Well, he's dead." The man barked out a laugh, and I flinched, and he thought that was funny too. "Been dead a good thirty years. His sister's boy owns the place. We just *call* him Coleman, that's all. It gets off with him."

"So I'll talk to *him* then. What's his real name?"

"His name is Buddy Durwood, but you won't find him around, not anytime soon. He's got him a new wife, and they went off gambling at one of them Indian gambling casinos up in North Carolina. Got him a wife looks like she ought to be out selling Girl Scout cookies, and Coleman — Buddy, I mean — he's sixty-six." He shook his head, kept wiping his greasy hands with that rag.

"So who's in charge?" I asked.

The man sat down on a car seat with a piece of cushion still attached to it. The seat was on top of a row of boxes beside the wall, and the other end of the car seat stuck up in the air, so the man sat at an angle, leaning to his left. He grabbed some rags off the floor, wadded them up, turned sideways, and stuck them under his head.

"Sit down," he said. "Something I want to tell you." He pointed at the chair beside the desk.

"So who's in charge?" I said. "We'll go to the police or the sheriff if that's what it takes to get our car back."

"Hold on now," he said, "I'm listening to you, I'm listening. I know y'all are tired of not having your car."

"So who's in charge?"

"Well, that's a good question," he said. "The truth is, nobody."

"Where's that big guy who drove the tow truck? Where's he?"

"Oh, that was Hubert. He quit the next day after your car come in, I believe. Got him a job up in Macon at the zipper factory."

"Well, how about you?" I said. "Can't you get our car fixed for us?"

"All right," he said, "I hear you. You not by yourself. I got other cars here too, you see." He waved a hand toward the back wall. "Other folks on my case too. One of them needed some tires, and so I had to swap out yours for theirs, only I was going to get you some better ones than the ones you started off with. So that's why your car's up on blocks."

"Those tires were worth a lot," I said. "You can't just 'swap them out.'"

He sat up, and the wad of rags he was using for a headrest fell on the floor beside the old car seat. "Tell you what," he said. "What if we do this? What if I let y'all borrow a car, just to get wherever you're going, and then we can swap it out for yours later on. I'll get somebody to bring it to you over at the motel. How about that?"

"That's not going to work," I said.

"Why not?" He stood up. "Come on out here, let me show you what we got."

We walked out back of the garage, into the junkyard, a sloping hillside of open hoods and crumpled bodies, most of the cars sitting on blocks or flat on the ground.

"These are here for parts, so don't pay no attention to them," he said. "I've got a good car for you and your mama over by the fence here."

It did look pretty good—a little white Toyota. He slammed his hand down on the hood. "Drive it off the lot right now," he said, amused with himself.

I told him we needed our car.

When I got back to the room, I told my mother what had happened. She was lying on the bed reading, which was how she spent most days now. She checked out books from the small library in Sabbath Creek.

"Right now, Lewis," she said, "if you want to know the truth, I don't care."

9

I stepped through the door of Stroud's place and took off my cap. The first time I had gone into his apartment with my cap on, he had snatched it off my head and handed it to me.

He was back in his bathroom on his knees, cleaning the tub. I could tell he'd already scrubbed the sink and toilet. "I'm just about done here," he said. "Give me a minute." He rinsed the tub, washed out his brush, and looped its cord over the showerhead.

I went out and sat at the big cherry-wood table, and I was looking at my reflection in the shine when Stroud came into the room.

"Cleanliness," he said, "is next to *what?*" He waited a beat. "Impossible. Next to impossible. It truly is. You leave that table alone, don't even touch it, don't do nothing to it, and in a few days, there'll be dust all over it, and I'll have to polish it again. Things get dirty on their own. You don't have to do nothing. What's on your mind, boy? I got things to do."

I told him I had talked to a man over at Coleman's. I laid my glove, ball, and cap—all folded into one—on the floor, not wanting to mess up the tabletop, and the cap dropped out.

"Where'd you get that cap?" He picked it up and looked it over, put it on his head and took it off and put it on again.

"Out back. In that pile of stuff."

"You better stay out of there," he said. "No telling what you might find, or what might find *you*. All kinds of rats and snakes in there, I know that. I'd clean it out myself if I was up to it. Cost too much to get it hauled off." He removed the cap and looked at it again. "Sure didn't have no idea this was back there, though. Huh. Look like you cleaned it up."

"Yes, sir. It was real dirty. What's the *S* for?"

"The Sabbath Creek Black Stars," he said, his voice rising on the word *Stars*. "The by-God *Stars*. Been a long time since I seen one of these. *Long* time. I had me a team, you see, semi-pro, back in the thirties. A little after that, too, but those were the best years. Teams would come through and stay here, and we'd play one game Saturday afternoon, usually, and one on Sunday afternoon. Except that was a problem sometimes. Some folks wouldn't play on Sunday, but we could still get up enough for a game."

"They stayed *here?*"

"What you mean 'They stayed *here?*' Boy, this was a fine place way back then. You don't know nothing about it. I had me a *good* business, a *fine* place for colored folk to stay. I had twelve good rooms. Half of them tore down now." He walked over to the window and pointed.

"You see that right there, where them wires come out the roof? That was a special suite. Two fancy rooms, a little kitchen, a private patio. Folks had their honeymoons there, some of them, and their anniversaries. It used to be *something,* going out to the Sabbath Creek Motor Court. And this place here?" He raised his arms. "This room, part of it, was a little cafe me and my wife had. She fixed it up just the way she wanted it. Served homecooking. Nothing fancy, but the best you ever had. She was some cook, my baby was. Best wife a man ever had, too."

"Was that your first wife?"

"First and only," he said. "Couldn't nobody take *her* place. Not ever. My sweet Ramona. Lord have mercy." He ran his fingers across the cap's top and turned it over.

"But I thought you had four wives. You told us you had four wives and outlived them all."

"See now," he said, "that was what everybody calls a white lie. A straight lie, no doubt about it, but then you call it white, see, and that makes it okay. So that was a white lie."

He stared at me and seemed to be waiting for me to say something, and when I didn't, he smiled and slapped me on the shoulder with the cap. "But look here, we had us a *team* in '38, though, what *I* mean. Played some of the Negro Leagues' professional teams, and we did all right. We did all right."

"Did you play?"

"Did I play? Boy, I was the reason we had the team. I mean, I could *bring* it back then. Had me some real heat. Struck out seventeen batters one game, didn't walk a one. Didn't throw nothing but smoke and a little change. And when I pulled the string, batters like to fell down."

"How did you get control?" I asked him. "I can throw hard, but I'm really wild."

"You got to figure that out for yourself," he said, and he handed me the cap. I tried to get him to keep it, but he wouldn't. He put his hands in his pockets.

I told him I worked on my control all the time, but it didn't get any better. I asked him if he'd help me.

"Well."

He pointed at my glove and ball. "Let me see your fastball grip," he said, and I showed him.

"You always hold it across the seams? Does it move?"

I told him I got a little rise on it sometimes, and that it would fade into a right-handed batter, but that I couldn't tell when that was going to happen.

"Look here," he said, reaching for the ball. "You got to have two things. Got to have control and then you got to have movement on the ball. Got to have them both. But if you don't have control, it don't matter how much movement you got. Look here. Grip it *across* the seams like you doing already—four-seam grip, you see, gives it a spin that you can count on. You grip it *with* the two seams, you don't know exactly how it's going to spin. You know it, but you can't be as sure, all right? You listening to me? So your grip is all right. You just got to make sure you keep it the same while you working on control. Got to keep your fingers the same width, got to have your thumb under the ball, on the same spot every time. You start moving that thumb, and the ball will sail on you, or sink, and that's fine for later on, when you get to the big leagues, but not for now. While you working on control, make everything *what?* The same. You got it?" He waited for me to answer.

"Yes, sir. Do you want to play catch?" I said. "And maybe you could show me some things?" But I did know that he was too old.

He sat there holding the ball, looking at it. He brought it to his nose and took a deep breath. He put his lips to the ball, pulled it back, and looked at it again. He opened his hand and let the ball rest on his open palm. He wrapped his thumb around it, his fingers still extended. He raised his hand, holding the ball with only his palm and his thumb.

"This here's my change grip," he said. "I just guide it with my fingers."

"So maybe we could throw some?" I asked him.

"Well."

He took a deep breath and let it out and coughed once. "Maybe. I don't know. Not today."

10

Somebody was walking outside our room. The footsteps went down toward the end of the motel, then came back and traveled past our door. I got up and peeked out through the edge of the curtains. Headlights shined straight at the window.

And then my mother was standing beside me, her left arm hugging her purse, where she kept the pistol, her right hand inside it. Her breath made a scraping noise in her throat.

The footsteps came back and stopped, a car door thumped shut, the headlights swung sideways, and our room went dark.

* * *

I found a Gideon on the shelf in our closet, but when I picked it up, the cover stuck to the wood and tore off, leaving me with a floppy bible that was hard to read.

I lay back on the bed, and it came over me again—that falling away—as I opened the book to Ecclesiastes:

> The eye is not satisfied with seeing, nor the ear filled with hearing. . . .
>
> all have one breath, so that a man hath no preeminence above a beast. . . .
>
> Better is the end of a thing than the beginning thereof. . . .

I tried to slam the book shut, but it had no cover and was hard to grip and it wouldn't slam, and I slung it sideways and it slid under the other bed.

11

Around nine o'clock one morning we heard banging and thumping next door, in the unoccupied Room Two. We heard a man's voice and then a woman's.

"That's all up to you, baby," she said, and we heard the bedsprings start to creak, slowly at first, then faster.

My mother pulled me out the door, and we walked around to Stroud's back entrance. When he opened the door, she said, "Excuse me, but may we come in? Our room is a bit too noisy at the moment because of the people next door."

"People next *door?* Ain't no people next door."

"Well then, you better go have a look for yourself. Somebody's definitely in the room next to ours, and they're making quite a bit of noise. Not the sort of noise I want my son listening to."

"I don't follow you."

"The *bed* is making noise."

"All right then," he said, "all right, I gotcha. May *be* somebody in that room then. Come on, y'all make yourself at home. I got bacon, toast, grits, got these special eggs, scrambled up with hot pepper sauce, make you want to slap your grandma. I got coffee, orange juice, prune juice—got a whole gallon of that—buttermilk, sweet milk, chocolate milk. Want some chocolate milk, son?"

"Yes, sir," I said. "Thanks."

"You welcome," he said. "And how about you, Miss America? What'll you have?"

Everything was already on the table—big bowls of eggs and grits, a platter of bacon, six pieces of toast. "Were you planning to eat all this yourself?" My mother picked up a strip of bacon and took a bite. "Good bacon."

Stroud said, "Thank you, ma'am," and he took her by the arm, pulled out a chair, and seated her at the place that was already set. "You sit there, son," he said, pointing to a chair across from my mother, "and I'll get us some plates."

It was the best food we had eaten in a very long time. My mother asked him where he'd learned to cook.

"Shoot. I been cooking since I could walk. All the children in our family had to cook. Just one of the things my mama and my grandma taught us all. There wasn't no sitting back and being waited on, no sir. It was mostly my grandma, though, that taught me how to cook. And she knew things don't nobody know these days, old things, from way back."

"Like what?" my mother asked.

Stroud chewed slowly and swallowed and wiped his mouth and took a drink of coffee. "Excuse me," he said. "Best to eat it while it's still hot. I'll tell you one thing Mama Dell—that's what everybody called my grandma, Mama Dell—one thing Mama Dell cooked up that you don't even hear about these days, and that's rock soup."

"Rock soup?" I asked.

"R-O-C-K soup," he said. "Rock. Like a rock off the ground. Mama Dell made rock soup. Some of the best soup you ever tasted, and good for you too. Good for your bones and teeth, you see. Made them hard, so they wouldn't break."

"So how did your grandma make this rock soup?" Mom asked him.

"Made it out of *rocks,*" Stroud said. "Used to send me and my brother Walter out to hunt for some good soup rocks. We knew how to pick them, you see. Didn't everybody know that. We'd bring in a load, Mama Dell would have us scrub them first with these special brushes she had, and then we'd soak them awhile in hot water, and then we'd scrub them again, this time with soap. Now that right there was the trick to cleaning your soup rocks. Use too much soap, that's all you taste. But if you don't use enough, it taste like dirt."

Stroud took another bite of eggs and grits, and he chewed very slowly.

"So how could you and your brother tell which rocks would make good soup and which wouldn't?" My mother sounded as though she were planning on making some rock soup herself.

"Glad you asked that," he said. "Look here. Some folks, you send them out to get rocks for soup, first thing they do is go down to the creek, pick out some rocks already clean and smooth. Now if you was to take them rocks in to Mama Dell, she'd send you right back out. No taste to them, for one thing, and all the strength done washed out of them, for another. You see, you got to dig *down* a little to get a good soup rock. Can't just pick it up off the ground or out of the creek. And a good soup rock's got a smell to it. It just smells right, you see. Hard to say exactly what the smell is. Walter used to say it was something like rain in the air, like the air when it's fixing to rain."

The eggs weren't hot at first, but they sneaked up on me and started to burn my mouth, and I had to gulp down some chocolate milk.

"You lucky I didn't cook up the *real* hot kind, like I usually do. Look here." He stood up, waved me over, and opened a cabinet, where he had two shelves of different kinds of hot sauces. I saw a bottle with a skull and crossbones on it, and the name *Death Penalty*. Another label showed a picture of a nearly naked woman; the sauce was called *Hot Bitch at the Beach*.

"I normally get me one of these and keep it beside me while I'm cooking, you see. Put it on everything. The truth is, though, some of these are too hot to eat, so hot they got no taste to them. All they do is burn. This one here." He took down a small, wide bottle filled with a reddish-black liquid. The label read *No Return*.

"This one here's the hottest they ever made. I used it *one* time, just *one* drop, and nearly died. I started hiccuping, couldn't breathe, and I drank a whole half-gallon of buttermilk, and even that didn't cut it. You got to drink milk, you see. If milk won't do it, nothing will. Cuts the oil. Water won't do you a bit of good."

I noticed that the bottle was about a third gone. "If you only used one drop, what happened to the rest of that stuff?"

"Well," he said, "what I do is, once or twice a year, I take a old toothbrush, put a drop on it, then I go along the bottoms of the doors, along the baseboards and the windows and the vents and any cracks I might find anywhere in the rooms. Won't nothing come across it. Ain't had a roach in years."

When we were finished eating, my mother asked him again, "So were you going to eat all this yourself?"

"No ma'am," he said, "I wasn't. Why don't y'all sit with me out on the porch a few minutes while I have me a cigarette?"

We went out, and Stroud offered my mother the chair he usually sat in, but she declined. He put on a cap that was lying in the chair, and he pulled the bill down low. I thought he looked funny. He said, "Laughing at a old man?"

"No, sir," I said.

"This here's my early morning hat, you see. I usually get out a little earlier, when the sun's just up. I like to sit here and watch it come through the pines and have me a smoke and think about things." He lit his cigarette, shook the pack so another one slid halfway out, and he offered it to my mother. "Smoke, young lady?"

"Why, thank you," she said. She pulled it from the pack and leaned over, and Stroud lit it. She saw me looking at her, and she said, "I'm just having a single cigarette, Lewis, that's all. I'm not about to start smoking."

"I done told the boy not to smoke," Stroud said. "Told him he won't be the ballplayer he *could* be if he starts smoking."

Stroud's air conditioner cut off. It was a loud window unit that extended out onto the patio, and when it was running, you had to speak up to make yourself heard over the roar. When it cut off, the silence seemed to rise up all around us.

Stroud pointed toward the trashpile on the other side of the fence. "Look yonder," he said. "See how the sun hits that busted glass right along in there?" We turned and saw light playing off the tangle of broken things.

"Yes, sir. Every day I fix me a good breakfast, then come out here, put on my thinking cap, smoke a little, and think about things."

"What kinds of things?" my mother asked.

"Well," he said, "mostly things from way back. What you *think* a old man's going to think about?"

"Come on, now," she said. "You're not that old."

"Not that *old?*"

"Well," she said, "I mean, you're . . ."

"Look here," Stroud said, "ain't nothing wrong with being old. I ain't ashamed of it. Folks use *old* like it was a cuss word. Don't even want to say it. They'll say, 'Oh, he's so many years *young.*' Look here. That's when you know you *really* old. Folks afraid to even *say* the word around you, scared you might seize up on them right there."

My mother asked him if he'd lived in Sabbath Creek all his life.

"Not yet."

"It's hard to get a straight answer out of you."

"Think so?" He gave her a real smile. "You sound like my wife, Ramona. She didn't pay no attention to half the things I said. Always calling me a old fool. She was right, I knew that, except I wasn't really old back then. I did cut the fool, though. But I ain't about to apologize for it, no sir. Better than being like a uncle I had, my Uncle Roebuck. Looked like he was mad all the time. Folks said Roebuck's face had a grip on it — that's the way they put it; made my mama laugh — said his face had a grip on it."

My mother tried again. "So were you born here?"

"Just down the road," he said. "Fourth of July, 1901. Everybody was drunk because of the holiday. Mama too. I was her ninth baby, the last one. She didn't have too much trouble with me, and her being drunk didn't hurt none, I imagine. The story went around that I was drunk too when I was born. Mama Dell swore I had whiskey on my breath when she held me, right after I was born."

"That couldn't really be true, could it?" I said. "Can a baby be drunk when it's born?"

Stroud just looked at me.

"Fourth of July," he said. "Time was, I threw a party every fourth, threw it for myself. Back when the Sabbath Creek Motor Court was big, folks from all over would book rooms just for the party. Man, we had some *times,* what *I* mean. Ramona, she would show out. She'd be cooking all week before the party. One year, they wrote about it in the paper up in Macon. When Satchel Paige was staying here."

He threw this out like it was nothing.

"Satchel *Paige?*" I said. "Stayed here?"

"Yes, sir," Stroud said. "More than once. Why? You think I'm lying?"

"No, sir," I said, "but I mean, Satchel Paige was so famous . . ."

"I can prove it if I got to," he said. "If that's the way you want to be, I can prove it to you. Let me finish my cigarette first, though. I don't want to carry it into the house." He took a drag on the cigarette in his right hand and put his left on the head of the lawn jockey beside his chair.

"Where'd you get that little statue?" my mother asked him.

"This boy?" He patted the statue's head. "I had him a long time. This here is Eugene. Eugene Talmadge."

My mother laughed, but I didn't see what was funny.

"Why do you call him that?" I asked.

"Because that's his name. What am I *supposed* to call him? Yeah, me and Eugene Talmadge here go way back. He's like a member of the family."

We went inside, and Stroud showed me an autographed

picture of Satchel Paige, but it looked like the kind you could get through the mail. He also had an autographed baseball, old and brownish-yellow, but the autograph said *Leroy Paige,* not *Satchel.*

"It says Leroy."

"That was his name," Stroud said. "Run get your glove, why don't you? We'll throw a little bit." He reached into a cabinet and pulled out an old glove with no webbing between the fingers, the kind of glove I'd only seen in pictures, more like the hand of a movie monster than a baseball glove.

"With that ball?"

"This ball not good enough for you? You too good to throw the same ball Satchel Paige had in his hand?"

"No, sir," I said. "I didn't mean that. But I thought maybe you wouldn't want to get it dirty."

"Why?" he said. "You plan on throwing it in the dirt?"

I went out the door, and they followed me onto the patio. When I looked back I saw my mother lighting another cigarette.

The door of the room next to ours was standing open. I figured the people had left. I went into our room and got my glove, came out and locked our door again, then stepped inside the other room. It looked a lot like ours did that first day. A bare mattress, a table with a broken leg lying sideways near the window, two lamps without bulbs or shades. The rug had a big burnt spot in it, round and about a foot wide, like somebody had once built a fire there. The door looked as though it had been kicked in and repaired. The walls were beaten up — dented and scratched and caved-in. Strips of wallpaper hung down. On the wall above the bed there was an old stain, a dark red splatter.

The mirror over the sink was gone, except for a single piece near the top that made a V-shape and angled out from the wall. The bathroom door was closed, and when I tried to open it, it moved only an inch or so, and I could see that the bathroom was filled with junk and trash. A hot stink hit me in the face, and I shut the door quickly. Going out, I took another look at the bed.

When I got back, Stroud was standing beside the patio, the glove on his left hand, the ball in his right. "You get lost?" he said.

"I was just looking around. Those people in the next room aren't there anymore, and I went in and looked."

"Find any evidence?"

"Evidence of what?"

"I don't know, boy. You the one snooping around. You tell *me*. You ready to throw?"

"I guess."

"You guess wrong," he said. "Did you get yourself loose? Did you do your stretches?"

"I feel all right."

"I didn't ask how you feel, son. I asked did you get yourself loose. Did you get yourself loose?"

I'd never had to warm up much at all, but I started stretching my arm and shoulder, making windmill motions backward and forward.

"Hold on," Stroud said. "Hold on. What you doing, boy?"

"Loosening up."

"Loosening up," he said. "That's what you call loosening up. Look here. You got to start with your legs. Got to start with your legs."

He showed me how to stretch my legs, then my back, and he

made me do it, and then he sent me off to run. "Give us about thirty minutes," he said. "Real slow, almost walking. I'll just sit here and talk with Miss America till you get back."

He told me to run a different route from the one I'd been taking. He said to go down the road toward the store and take the first left. It was a dirt road I'd passed but never followed.

"Got a hill or two up that way," he said. "No traffic."

12

The dirt road snaked upwards in a series of switchbacks, straightened out into one long incline, then hooked downhill to the right. The trees were suddenly thicker, and somewhere below, not far off, a dog started barking, then several dogs, and then I saw them and heard them running toward me—a scuffling, gasping sound. They didn't bark as they ran, but gave out deep growls, holding their heads low, and they came at me hard. I stopped running, reached down and picked up a rock, and the dogs leapt backwards and started barking again, spread out and surrounded me. I walked backwards, and they barked louder and came closer. The biggest one lunged at me, and I threw the rock and missed, and the dog jumped back and circled left, its wide head low, its odd gray eyes glistening, fixed on my face. The two smaller dogs—both a dirty white, their hair patchy and thin—feinted runs at me, but stayed back. The big dog stopped circling and bared his teeth, and I could see the shoulder muscles working under his dark coat streaked with black, the color of old blood. I backed into the ditch, the dog came at me, and I picked up a stick and swung it, but it was rotten and soft and it broke, and the dog came closer.

And then I heard a sound I couldn't place, a rumbling noise, and I saw a tractor rounding the curve, a girl driving it. She revved the engine, and it gave a loud pop and made a whirring noise followed by a clank, and she shouted, "If you don't bother them, they won't hurt you."

"Are they your dogs?" I shouted back.

She cut the engine and jumped down from the tractor and walked quickly toward the dogs. "Come here, boys." She got on her knees and they surrounded her, and she pulled them close and kissed the big one on his head. "Cat, you bad thing. Were you scaring this boy? Were you?"

"I wasn't scared," I said, but I heard my voice.

"Well, I'm sorry if they got in your way. They make a lot of racket, but they've never hurt anybody. They're sweethearts. Aren't you, Mr. Perkins?" She rubbed the back of one of the smaller dogs, both of which had sidled up next to her.

I took a step backwards, and the big dog, the one she'd called Cat, turned and growled, and the girl grabbed his collar. "He really won't hurt you. I promise. Where are you going, anyway?"

"Nowhere," I said. "I was just out running. My mother and I are staying up here at the Sabbath Creek Motor Court, waiting for our car to get fixed. We live in Cofield."

"I didn't know that old motel was even open anymore. The man who runs it was sick and in the hospital, and I thought they shut down."

"You mean Stroud?" I said.

"Yeah, I guess that's his name. I don't know him, but my mother does."

"What was he in the hospital for?"

"Who knows?" she said. "It could be anything, as old as he is. That place looks really filthy. I don't know how you can stand to stay there."

She told me to come closer and let the dogs get used to me, so I walked carefully to where she was kneeling. "Give me your cap," she said. I handed it to her, and she let all the dogs sniff it. "They need to get used to your smell. Now rub Cat's back."

I reached over and rubbed the dog's back, though I didn't want to, and I asked her what kind of dog he was.

"I'm not sure. I think he's got some pit bull in him, though."

I shifted from a kneeling to a sitting position, and when I did, the dog growled again.

"So do you live down this road?" I asked the girl.

She said, "You want to see where I live?" She didn't wait for an answer. She got up and walked to the tractor and told me to jump on, and we drove downhill and around a curve, and then I could see a house beside a pond, an expanse of smooth silver water reflecting the clouds.

She invited me into the house and offered me a soft drink.

She said her mother was a doctor and her stepfather managed other people's money, and neither one spent much time at home. I told her I had thought maybe they were farmers, because of the tractor. They only used it for their garden, she said, and to cut the grass, and when her parents were gone she liked to drive it up and down the road in front of the house, which they'd forbidden her to do. But they'd been having such a vicious fight for the last few days, she said, she could probably drive it to Florida and they wouldn't even notice.

"The tractor's sort of a running joke between my parents. Donald, my stepfather, bought it and pretended he was actually going to use it, but he knows nothing at all about farming.

My mother knows a little, but not much. What do your folks do?"

I told her that my father was a bookkeeper at a cotton mill and that my mother wrote for a newspaper in Cofield.

"And you're staying at that old motel, waiting for your car to get fixed? Who's fixing it?"

"A place called Coleman's."

She said someone should have warned us about Coleman's. Everybody knew they were incompetents and crooks.

"That's what Stroud told us. I went over to see about the car, and they'd sold the tires. I told the man they'd better find us some more tires and get the car running, or I'd report them to the sheriff or the police or somebody."

"Couldn't your father drive down and pick you up? You'll never get anything out of those folks at Coleman's."

We stood in the kitchen while she fixed our drinks. She handed me the glass and led me into a room with tall windows, polished hardwood floors, a wide fireplace with a stone hearth.

"Let's sit here," she said, and she flopped down onto the short sofa and turned sideways, her knee almost touching my leg. She asked me how old I was.

"Fourteen," I said, since it was almost my birthday.

"I just turned fifteen," she said, though she looked older.

I asked her what her parents had been fighting about.

"Oh, it's not over yet," she said. "Since *I am* still here, and *I* seem to be the problem. The problem is little Eva, which is what my stepfather likes to call me, as if no one else had ever thought of that. He thinks he's so clever, he just can't help himself."

When I got ready to go, she offered to drive me out to the highway on her tractor, but I told her I'd run. She said, "Okay then, I'll run out there with you," which was fine with me, except that I had a hard time keeping up.

13

Stroud said, "Where you been, boy? People got things to do, don't you know that? You get lost?"

I told them about the dogs and the girl on the tractor, and I started to say more, but Stroud wasn't interested in hearing it; he was tired of waiting.

"Look here," he said, "let's get your arm loose. Hold it out here."

I held out my arm and he squeezed the muscles, felt the bones, pinched and poked at my elbow, moved my wrist up and down, bent my fingers back and forth, and he made me do a set of stretches. Then finally he stood up and flipped me a ball, but it wasn't the one signed by Satchel Paige. We'd start off with a newer ball, he said, and we could throw the other one later.

"Let's just lob a few now," he said. He was about forty feet away when I tossed him the ball, and he stabbed at it with his glove, as though he were trying to knock the ball down, but he caught it. I was surprised that the ball stayed in that old glove, as bulky as it was and with its fingers fanning out.

His return throw had no spin—a knuckleball—and as I reached to catch it, it dipped sharply, hit the heel of my glove, and fell to the ground.

"You let me know if I need to go easy on you, son." Stroud stepped back and hitched up his pants. "We can start slow."

I lobbed the ball again, and he came back with another knuckler, but I was ready for it and caught it, though it broke sideways at the last instant.

"So you were a knuckleball pitcher?"

"*Knuckleball* pitcher? Just because I can throw the wobbly?"

I tossed him the ball, and he walked toward me, came up and put his hand on my shoulder, stood close and spoke in a low voice, like a catcher having a conference with his pitcher. His breath smelled like cigarettes and peppermint.

"Look here," he said. "When I was right, not even Leroy Paige threw harder than I did. Don't get me wrong—he was a better pitcher, a thousand times better than me—but when it come to speed, you see, I had as much as he did. So no, I wasn't no *knuckleball* pitcher. I didn't throw no trash. I was quick. I just like to play with it, that's all. I threw hard enough to get in the big time, I really did, and if there was anybody left to *tell* you that, they'd tell you."

He turned around, and he stepped off the distance. "This looks about right," he said, "but we need us a home plate." He put down his glove to mark the spot, and he walked over to the patio and lifted the ashtray from the lawn jockey's head.

I told him it was too little, but he said it was good to have a small target.

"When Leroy was a boy, he used a lid off a mason jar, and then later on, a case quarter. That's how he got his control. People say one time he bet a man fifty dollars he could put out a candle without touching the candlestick. The man said he'd give him three tries, and Leroy said he didn't need but one. Threw his B ball one time and cashed in. They say he could shave the icing off a cake."

Stroud leaned down and replaced the glove with the ashtray. "Can you see that?"

"Yes, sir. But what's a B ball?"

He threw me another knuckler. It didn't spin, but it didn't move either. "Uh oh," he said. "Somebody done hit that one *out*, what *I* mean."

After we'd thrown easily for a while, he said, "Put something on it this time. You throwing like a old lady."

I delivered the ball at about half speed, and he whipped it back to me. "I *said* put something on it, son. You got more than that, don't you?"

I knew he was too old to catch a real fastball, and so I gave him a three-quarter-speed pitch. He fired it back so hard it almost got by me. "Look here," he said, "I'm ninety-three years old. See can you throw as hard as me, why don't you?"

I threw him my good fastball, and it sailed high, and he had to go up on his toes to catch it. "That's it," he said. "Bring it on in here." I threw another hard one. "Now you got it," he said. "Had a little hop on it. Let's just throw now. You can throw without talking, can't you?"

For the next ten minutes, we fired the ball back and forth. Stroud caught everything I threw, but I dropped the knuckleball twice.

"So what's a B ball?" I finally asked again.

"What's a *B* ball?" He made it sound like I'd asked a silly question. "That was Leroy's name for a ball that's going to *be* where you want it to be. That's all. Look here. Leroy had all kinds of pitches. What he called his trouble ball, his jump ball, his quickie, his four-day rider, and his midnight creeper. Threw overhand, sidearm, and underhand. But most every pitch, whatever he called it, was a fastball. Batters used to joke that Leroy had "fastball" printed out on his left shoe, so you could see it when he raised his leg winding up. You knew what was coming, and it didn't make no difference, you still couldn't touch it. They said the ball changed *size,* what *I* mean. Looked like a marble coming in there."

I asked Stroud if Satchel Paige taught him how to throw any of those pitches.

"Well, one or two. One or two. That wobbly I been throwing at you. He taught me that. But Leroy didn't play much when he stayed here."

Stroud took off his glove, walked over to the patio, and flopped down in his chair. My mother had been sitting there watching us the whole time. I didn't know how much of our conversation she'd overheard, but now he was talking to her as much as he was to me.

"Leroy was here two times, you see, and he was like two different men. First time, 1937. He was thirty-one, and I was thirty-six. And that's another thing. All this mess about how old the man was. Wasn't ever no big mystery. Born in 1906. Even had him a *birth* certificate. Lots of *white* folks didn't even have that, not back then. That was all publicity, that's all it was—folks trying to make him some kind of clown in a sideshow. The man knew exactly how old he was. First time he come through, 1937, he was Satchel Paige. Next time, 1938, he was Leroy."

"I don't understand," I told him.

"Under*stand?* Ain't no *reason* for you to understand, son. I ain't explained it to you yet, all right?"

"Yes, sir."

"Slow down. I'll get to it."

"Yes, sir."

Stroud turned to my mother and said, "How about we fire up a Kool? What you say?" She shook her head. "How about a cool drink then? It's about that time."

"Are you having something?" she asked.

"I believe I will. Let's go in here and see what we got." He opened the back door, held it for her, then went in. I followed them, and we sat at the kitchen table, drinking iced tea that was cold and almost too sweet.

"So here's what happened with Leroy, son. That was his name, the one his mama gave him. He went back to it — at least that's what he told *me* to call him — for a while in 1938, when his arm went dead. Couldn't hardly raise his arm over his head, much less throw his jump ball. See, he'd never had no trouble with his arm at all, not ever. He said that was because of how he warmed up — lots more than most folks did — and how he cooled down. Took a real hot bath in the morning, water almost boiling, and another one after the game. He never threw until he'd done some running, fielded bunts and ground balls, chased flies. He kept his legs and back in shape, and that gave him good balance, that and not having no fat on his body. And he had other things, like this snake oil he'd rub on his arm. Some Indians gave it to him somewhere along the road, somewhere like South Dakota, I believe. They used it for snakebites and they said it was too hot for anything else, but Leroy didn't have no problem with the heat. The hotter the better, he said, and he kept some of it in a jar and used it after every game."

"Was it made out of snakes?" I asked.

"Could have been, for all I know. He just called it snake oil. You want to hear the story or not?"

"Yes, sir. I'm sorry."

"Well," he said. He rattled the ice cubes in his glass, then stood and got the tea pitcher out of the refrigerator. "How about you, Miss America?" My mother lifted her glass, and the old man filled it again. He poured some for himself and then for me. When he opened the refrigerator door to put the pitcher back, I noticed a shelf full of medicine bottles, and I remembered what Eva had said about Stroud having been in the hospital.

"Were you in the hospital?" I asked him.

"Yes, sir, I was indeed." he said. "Mental hospital up in Milledgeville. I got a piece of paper that shows I ain't crazy no more. You want to see it?"

"No, sir."

I never thought Eva meant he was in a mental hospital. Stroud looked as serious as I'd ever seen him, and then when he sat back down, he glanced over at Mom, and he burst out laughing and then coughing, and he pulled out his handkerchief and stood up and coughed and laughed into it.

After a moment, he said, "Man, that was a good one. You should have seen your face, boy. Like I was a ghost. Come out the *mental* hospital." He grabbed me as he said this, and I jumped, and that set him off again, and he laughed and wheezed a few times, then stepped to the sink and washed his face.

"Man alive," he said, shaking his head. He sat in the chair and slid down, his feet stretched out, his hands flat on the table.

"How'd you know I was in the hospital? You get that from the little girl down the road? She tell you that?"

I nodded, and he said, "Folks know everything, don't they?" And he smiled at my mother. "All right then, back to Leroy. He kept real good care of his arm, always stayed in shape, warmed up good, got loose, cooled down right, rubbed his arm with snake oil, and so on. But he had some problems, you see, mainly with his stomach, what he called the miseries. Sometimes it just doubled him up. He'd go on and pitch anyway—he felt like he owed it to the folks that came out to see him—but he got pretty bad off sometimes, to where he couldn't eat nothing but boiled chicken and fish. My wife Ramona fixed him up the best plate of bland food he ever ate, no spices or nothing, nothing off that shelf yonder,"—he pointed to the cabinet with all the hot sauces—"you can believe *that*. Anyhow, so one day when he was off in Mexico, his stomach got to hurting him real bad, worse than it ever had. The pain started to spread all over his body and pretty soon it got to his arm. It burned, and it felt like somebody had pinched off the blood. After a few days, he couldn't lift it, and then after awhile, his arm went dead. Couldn't hardly put his shirt on. He came back to America and went to the doctor, and they told him he wouldn't ever pitch another game as long as he lived. His arm was dead for good, they said. When he stayed here the second time, in 1938, you see, that was when his arm was dead. He came down here for Ramona to cook for him, thinking maybe it would help his arm, but it didn't. And when he was here that time, he wouldn't let nobody call him Satchel. Wherever his arm had gone, the famous Satchel Paige had gone with it, he said. He said call him Leroy, like his mama did. So we called him Leroy, and I still do."

My mother asked, "Did he get better, though, eventually?"

"What you mean 'Did he get better?' You don't know about Satchel Paige? Pitched on up into his sixties. Only man in the world that's ever done anything like that. He got better, all right, but not while he was here. You never seen a man as down and out as Leroy Paige that month he stayed with us. He did heal up some, I know that, but when he left, he still couldn't raise his arm."

"Did you know any other famous players?" I asked him.

"Well," Stroud said, "not to speak of. Not really. I played a few innings with Cool Papa one time. That's about it."

"Cool Papa Bell?"

"No." Stroud studied my face closely. "Cool Papa Rockefeller. How many Cool Papas you know about?"

"I'm sorry," I said.

"Ain't no need to be sorry, boy. Just think a little, that's all. Use your head."

14

Stroud said a man had called the motel and asked if a woman and a boy were staying there. Stroud asked him who wanted to know, and the man said, "I might be her husband."

"I said, 'You *might* be *any*body, Jack. Don't matter who you are, husband or not, we don't talk about folks staying here.' That's what I said to him, but then I went on and told him no, there was nobody here at all. I asked him why was he calling me and wasting my time."

"Did he say anything else?" my mother asked.

"He was about to hang up, and I asked him where he was calling me from, and he said he was over at McRae. I told him, 'Whoever you looking for, they ain't here,' and I hung up on him."

15

Two days later, I ran back out to Eva's house, but this time nobody was there, not even the dogs. I knocked on the door, then went down to the little boathouse beside the lake, but nobody was there either. I walked up onto the deck and knocked, then I tried the glass door and it slid open. I leaned inside and called Eva's name, then shut the door and sat on one of the deck chairs and waited. I took the little fish out of my pocket and I was looking at it when I heard the door slide open behind me, and Eva came out. I felt really strange, sitting on her deck without having been asked. I told her I was resting up before running back to the motel. She said she was glad I came, and she asked me what I had in my hand. I held out the carving, and she took it.

"I've got one just like this," she said.

I told her I'd bought it at Furlow's, and I carried it as a good-luck charm, even though I didn't really believe in such things. I repeated what the girl at Furlow's had said about the man who carved it.

"He's not retarded, though," Eva said. "She's wrong about that. He was injured in the Vietnam War. His name is Albert McGrath. His face was mangled and burned and his brain was damaged, and it's a miracle he's still alive. The first time I saw him, it really scared me, he just looked so awful. I didn't want to be scared, but I couldn't help it. Mom says he's got more reason to be afraid of other people than they have to be afraid of him. He's not going to hurt anybody—he's completely harmless—but he looks like a monster. I hate to say it, but he really does. Mom says all the doctors in the area know about him, since he's been treated up at the veterans' hospital in Dublin, and somebody wrote an article about him in a big medical journal. She says he's a really unusual case."

She gave back the fish, and I put it in my pocket. We went inside, and she heated some leftover pizza in the microwave, poured us each a glass of lemonade, and we took our food back out onto the deck.

"I was thinking I'd be met by your dogs again, and I was hoping they'd remember me," I said, "but I didn't see them."

"They weren't really my dogs, I guess. Donald took them with him when he left. That happened yesterday."

"Your parents split up?"

"Yeah," she said, "but I've been through it before. It's not that big a deal. My real dad left when I was four. That was the worst. That was really, really bad. Old Donald was my mother's third husband, and they've only been married a year. He brought the dogs with him. I'll miss them a lot more than I'll miss him, that's for sure."

"I guess your mother must be pretty upset."

"Not really," she said. "I don't think Mom ever actually liked Donald very much. I think she married him because he was available and attractive and he made a good living, and she didn't think he'd get in the way. She was wrong about that, though."

"Where did he go?"

"Oh, he already had another house, a rental property up in Macon, and he moved there. Told the people living there they'd have to get out. I don't know how he can do that, but I guess he can. He thinks he can order people around."

It was a strangely cool summer morning, almost like fall. The breeze caught a few strands of Eva's long brown hair, blew them across her face, and she flipped them away. She had a little bit of tomato paste, just a dot, beside the right corner of her mouth.

"I thought you'd be gone by now," she said. "Don't you feel kind of silly, staying at that old motel so long? Especially when you can be pretty sure nobody's really trying to fix your car?"

"Well, yeah."

Eva reached up and gently moved the hand I'd been holding to my face, partially covering my big nose.

"Look," she said, pointing toward the pond. "Those are my ducks."

Two ducks swam away from us, one behind the other, pulling a dark wake across the bronze water. "Only they're not really mine either, I guess."

"Hold still," I said, and I reached over with my napkin and wiped the bit of tomato paste from the corner of her mouth. "Mom and I left home because of my dad. That's why we're driving around."

"Why didn't she make *him* leave?"

"Well, she said she didn't want him to know where we were. She wanted to be in control of things. She said that if we stayed at home, he might just show up."

The ducks turned, made an arc near the middle of the small pond, and headed back to shore, and Eva leaned over and kissed me, and her mouth was soft, and I kissed her and wondered if she thought I was doing it right, and then I stopped thinking.

* * *

That afternoon, I ran down the road to the old house and threw at my taped-up strike zone. The stadium rose all around me, a closed canyon of shirts, three tiers with no empty seats. The crowd chanted and stomped, and the noise erupted in waves. It was the seventh game of the World Series, bottom of the ninth. We were ahead by one, but the other team had loaded the bases with two outs. The manager handed me the ball. The other team's best hitter dug into the batter's box. He rarely struck out, a real contact hitter. He crowded the plate. The best eyes since Ted Williams, people said. Uncanny bat control. He could foul the ball right or left or behind him at will.

Eva was in the stands.

I got my signal, shook it off, then went with the next one—a fastball, outside—and I paused in the stretch, then coiled and stepped and released, and the ball whacked the side of the old house four feet wide of the tape and a foot too high—a pitch that would have gone behind the batter and all the way to the backstop. I imagined it taking an unusual bounce, straight back into the catcher's hands, so that no one advanced.

I threw again, this time into the dirt, and my catcher made a great stop. I threw again—ball three. And then I heard Eva call my name, I heard her whisper above the stomping crowd, and I felt the blood rush through my muscles and bones, and I turned and let go with my best fastball, and it hit the house on the first bounce, nowhere near the tape.

I decided that none of it had happened, and I started again. Seventh game, last of the ninth, bases loaded, two outs, and we were one run ahead. And I threw one strike but walked the batter again, then another. Again, I erased history and started over, still as wild as I'd ever been.

Finally, I lay down in the grass, my glove under my head. I spread my arms out, ran my palms lightly over the tips of the weeds, then moved them deeper, so the weeds slowed me down and held me. I broke a stem near the root, brought it to my nose and breathed in, brushed it across my lips. The clouds, white as a new baseball, looked like nothing, took no shapes. They stayed still, fixed against the blue, but closer. And it made me dizzy, and I couldn't make it out, how close the clouds were, how far from the blue, or where exactly the blue was.

16

My mother asked Stroud if anybody visited him in the hospital, and he said he'd had two visitors, his niece and the preacher from the church down the road, and he could have done without either.

"There's nobody left," he said. "My niece, Josephine Young, but I don't really count her."

"Did you have a large family?" my mother asked him. "I remember you said you were the ninth child, but did you and your wife have children?"

"Let me show you," he said. "Stay right there." He stepped into the next room and returned with a framed photograph. "I keep this beside my bed, and I look at it every night before I go to sleep and every morning when I get up. Me and Ramona and the baby, little Truman Jr. He wasn't even a year old then. We called him Tru."

"Is he your only child?" my mother asked.

"Was. He's gone too. Been gone a long time, longer than his mama. It's hard to believe, but if he was alive today, he'd be a old man too."

He looked over at me and said, "Come here, boy," then reached down and picked up the baseball that was lying on the floor beside him. "Let me show you something Leroy taught me."

He showed me how to move the position of my thumb so it was more directly under the ball. He said if I released it the same as my regular fastball, it would sink.

"Puts a overspin on it, you see. It won't feel right at first, but you'll get used to it. Got to get your control first, though. Remember that."

I asked Stroud if his son had played ball.

"Did he *play?* Look here. He hit a ball so hard one time, they stopped the game so they could measure it. Four hundred eighty-six feet. He wasn't but sixteen years old. Jackie Robinson never hit a ball that far. Leroy saw Tru play when he was just a boy and said he was one of the best he'd ever seen."

"Did he play pro ball?" I asked him.

"He would have," Stroud said. "I do believe that, I believe he would have. But he was killed in the war, son. A shell caught him in the head, and when they shipped him home, you couldn't stand to look at him. Ramona made the folks show him to her, though. I told her it was a bad idea, fought with her about it, but she went on anyway. I looked at him too, and I can see it now like it was yesterday. No face. No head, really, just a stump of meat, like you'd see in a butcher shop. Ramona screamed like she'd been set on fire, reached over in there and tried to drag him up into her arms, and I had to pull her back, and we both went outside and got sick."

"I'm so sorry," my mother said. "I can't even imagine it."

Stroud said, "No, you really can't."

17

I asked Stroud why the town was called Sabbath Creek, since there was no creek.

"Look here," he said. "Just because you hadn't seen a creek don't mean there's not a creek. It runs west of town. I don't guess you been out there."

Years ago, he said, churches used the creek for baptisms. There was a large clearing and a sandbar where both black and white churches gathered to baptize people who'd been saved, and that's how the creek got its name.

"Not fit for much at all these days, though," he said. "There's a chicken processing plant upstream that dumps in feathers and blood and who knows what else."

* * *

One of the books my mother checked out of the library was an atlas that traced all of human history, using maps to show how the world had changed over time.

From the first page I was amazed, and for a while I enjoyed the book as though I were a normal person, but soon the atlas held me inside it as surely as it held the black ox drawn on a cave wall or a photo of a terra cotta man two thousand years old, and I imagined the impossible: we would all be dead forever, though forever would end.

The book closed itself in my hands.

Stroud and I were throwing a ball back and forth when he asked me about my father. He wanted to know why we were running away. I told him we were not running away. He said we could call it whatever we wanted, but it looked like running away to him. He wanted me to tell him what was wrong.

"It's just a family thing," I said, throwing the ball a bit faster. He snagged it and fired it back.

I threw the ball in the dirt, and Stroud made me chase it. It skipped across the gravel drive and rolled back into the trees. I picked up the ball, and then I heard a car, and I turned and saw a big silver Chrysler coming along the drive. The car zoomed right up to the edge of the yard and skidded to a stop with its front wheels on the grass. The door on the driver's side swung open, but nobody got out.

I walked past the other side of the car and into the yard. I still couldn't see the driver because of the glare off the windshield. Stroud had evidently gone inside—I didn't see him in the yard anymore—and so I'd headed that way to let him know he had company, when I heard a voice.

"Young man."

I turned and saw an old black woman standing beside the car.

"Would you be so kind as to help me with these packages?"

"Yes, ma'am," I said, and I hurried toward her. She looked unsteady on her feet, and when I reached the other side of the car, I saw that she was leaning on a walker.

"Those two right there, please." She nodded in the direction of two small plastic grocery bags on the seat. She turned away from the car, placed the walker behind her, and took two very slow steps. I reached in and picked up the bags and then shut the door. The woman planted the walker ahead of her and took two more steps. With each movement forward, she took a brief rest.

"I'll go get Stroud if you want me to," I told her.

She smiled at me, and with some difficulty she let go of the walker and laid a hand on my arm. "Oh, Uncle Truman knows I'm here. You can be certain of that. He's simply gone into what I call his tortoise mode. He's pulled into his shell for protection." She placed the walker again, tested it, and stepped. "You'd never guess I was once quite athletic, would you? At least one lifetime ago. Still, I've only been using this thing for a year." She jabbed the walker into place ahead of her and stepped again. I wondered where Stroud was. When she reached the back door, I started to open it for her, and she said in a whisper, "I'd better knock." She rapped on the door, pushed it open a little, and called out, "Uncle Truman, are you home?" I expected her to continue into the apartment, but she remained where she was, the door slightly ajar.

"Hello? Uncle Truman, it's Josephine. Are you decent?"

We stood and waited. The woman said, "He does this. It's one of his little games. He'll be here shortly."

And she was right. We waited maybe a minute, and then Stroud opened the door. He didn't say a word. He nodded a greeting and held the door while she made her way across the kitchen and into the next room, where she sat in a rocking chair. Stroud followed her, and I put the two bags on the kitchen table and walked into the small den where they were now both seated.

Stroud told me to go back to the kitchen and put the milk into the refrigerator. "I know she got milk in there," he said.

The woman looked at me and said, "Please."

I went in and put the food away, then came back and sat on the sofa.

"Uncle Truman, aren't you going to introduce me to this young gentleman?"

Stroud took a deep breath, then puffed out his lips as he released it, and he looked at me with tired eyes. "Son," he said, "this old woman is Miss Josephine Young, my wife sister girl. She ain't never been married. She taught school for a 129 years, and so she know what the answer is before you even ax the question." He looked at the old woman. "This boy Lewis and his mama stay up in Cofield. They been renting a room because they car broke down and they took it to that trash over at Coleman, where can't nothing good happen to it, and so they still here and look like they plan on being here the rest of they life. Unless the boy daddy come to get them. Him and his mama driving around to stay away from him. They might be serial killers, too, but they ain't tried to kill *me* yet."

Stroud was putting on a show—he didn't usually talk this way, and his voice had gone high and raspy.

"It's good to meet you, Lewis. And let me give you some advice, if you don't mind. Should you and your mother actually *be* ruthless killers, and should you intend to relieve this one of his mortal coil," — she pointed leisurely at Stroud — "you'll need to take extreme measures. There is some evidence that he has made a pact with the devil, and that he will indeed live forever."

Stroud stood up while she was talking, walked into the kitchen, and returned with three cans of Coke.

"So Lewis," Miss Young said, "where do you live?"

"They stay up in Cofield," Stroud said. "I done told you that. His daddy work for a mill up there. His mama work for a newspaper. Lewis, he a ballplayer, and he sit around reading the dictionary like a egghead."

"I was talking to the *boy*, Uncle Truman," Miss Young said, without looking at him. "Cofield is a lovely little town. I had a friend there once."

"Who was it?" I asked her.

"Oh, I doubt that you would know her. She's gone now."

"He *might* know her," Stroud said. "She was probably white. Give the boy a chance. I bet he know a lot of old white women."

"Uncle Truman." Miss Young seemed upset for the first time. "My friend wasn't white. It would not matter in the least if she *had* been, but she was not. Please stop talking that way — and in that ridiculous voice — in front of this boy."

"Stop *talking* that way? What you mean? This is *my* home, woman. I'll talk any damn way I want to in it. You don't like it, you can leave the way you came in. You got that?"

"I'll leave when I'm ready, sir," she said, "and not before that, thank you. The fact that you own the property doesn't allow you to suspend all considerations of civility."

"You hear that?" Stroud said to me. "She still teaching school. Suspend all this and that. She still teaching school."

"Perhaps I am, Uncle Truman. But I'm not ashamed of it in the least."

They both fell silent. I heard the fast wheeze of Stroud's breath. Miss Young repositioned herself in the rocker, pushing herself more upright, and the wood gave a sharp crack.

"What did you teach?" I asked her.

"Primarily high-school English, Lewis. I began as a first-grade teacher but then moved to high school, and I'd still be teaching today if I were mobile enough. I have the energy, and my mind is as sharp as ever." She looked at Stroud, as if expecting him to respond, but he didn't.

"I like English," I said.

"Look here, old woman, is there something you wanted? I got things to do. I can't be sitting around here all day."

"Well, now, that's what you do *every* day, isn't it? I don't believe you've gone out more than twice since I brought you home from the hospital. You have someone waiting on you hand and foot, and I am that someone."

"Look here," he said, "one reason I ain't been nowhere is you like to scared me to death on that ride home." He looked at me. "She ain't got *no* business on the road, that's one thing I know. She ain't driving the car, son, she *aiming* it. You see that big boat coming down the road, you better hit the ditch."

"Uncle Truman. It's true that my eyes are not what they once were. But you could at least show some gratitude. If I didn't bring you things, who would? Who else would put up with such abuse?"

Stroud settled back in his chair. "Did you bring the cornmeal like I told you? I bet you forgot it." He turned to me. "She always forget something. I call up and give her the list, and she say she writing it down, but then when she get over here, guess what she done did? Went and forgot it. Now how you going to forget it if you wrote it down? Tell me that."

"I brought the cornmeal."

"But did you get the store brand, like I told you?" He leaned over, as if he were telling me a secret. "What she *want* to buy, see, is that Martha *White* cornmeal. Can't get that, she'll buy *White* Lily. Anything white, she got to have it."

"They were out of the store brand, Uncle Truman, so I did indeed buy Martha White. I suppose it will, in your mind, produce some kind of Caucasian cornbread, but you'll just have to make the best of it."

Nobody spoke for a moment. Stroud turned and looked toward the kitchen, and Miss Young inspected the front of her blouse. I looked at the photo hanging behind Stroud. It was a tall man in a baggy baseball uniform. I recognized the cap on his head, exactly like the one I'd pulled from the trashpile out back, and I pointed at the photo.

"Who's that?"

"That?" Stroud said. "Son, that right there's one of the best shortstops ever played the game of baseball. Named Rabbit Dixon. Got his name because of how he went in the hole, you see. Had a better arm than anybody on the team, me included. Rabbit Dixon. Now, Rabbit was peculiar. Claimed he was not a Negro, no sir. One time I heard him say he was 'half white, half colored, and half Indian.' I told him it was too bad he didn't have some Chinese in there, or he could've played two positions at the same time. He acted like he didn't get it."

Miss Young laughed at that, and Stroud leaned over toward the old woman and said, "Needed him some Chinese, you see. Could've played two positions."

There were photos all over the walls, and many of them were men in baseball uniforms. I pointed at another one.

"Who's this?"

It was a picture of a very thin young man whose cap was too big. His ears stuck out, he looked surprised by the camera, and he appeared to be saying something as the photo was snapped, so his mouth was twisted sideways.

"He's funny looking," I said.

Miss Young let out a subdued whoop. "Whom does it resemble?" she said.

I studied the picture more closely, and I finally saw that it was Stroud, a good seventy years younger.

"Man," I told him, "you sure were skinny."

"How you like them ears?" he asked me. "How Ramona ever got past them jug handles, I'll never know." He looked at Miss Young, and she said nothing, but she did smile.

19

"At least you've had a real father," Eva said. She put her mouth against my neck and kissed me under the ear, and I wanted to say something, but I was afraid my voice would warble or choke up. She stopped kissing me, and she sat back and took my hand.

"So where's your real dad now?" I managed to ask her.

The ducks had come up onto the shore, and they looked slow and clumsy, waddling around. Their heads looked small, and their feathers were a dull gray.

She laid her head on my shoulder. "That's the worst part," she said. "He's got another family now, a girl and a boy. They live down near Miami. I go visit him three or four times a year, but it always makes me sad. I get jealous. I know it's stupid to feel that way, but I do anyhow. I'm sure they're all pretty glad when I leave, even my dad, though he'd never admit it."

The telephone rang. It was her mother, checking on her. "Everything's fine," she said. "No, I'm okay, really." She listened for a moment, then looked at me and made a silly face — puffed up her cheeks and made her eyes bulge out.

"All right then," she said. "I under*stand,* Mom, okay? I'll be fine. And yes, I practiced, but when are you going to get the piano tuned? You keep putting it off. It sounds terrible." She listened, her eyes flat, until finally she said, "Oh, by the way.

That boy I told you about? The one staying at the old motel on the highway? Well, he's here."

She looked at me and smiled. "He just came to see me, that's all. We had pizza and . . . but *why*, Mom? We were just talking. No, he's *younger* than I am. Okay, Mom," she said, her voice rising, "have it your way. I'll tell him to get out. Who needs friends anyhow? I'll be here all by myself till you decide to come home. Great. Goodbye." She hung up the phone hard.

I told her I didn't want to cause any trouble, and I stood up to go, but she grabbed my hand and pulled me back down onto the sofa.

"What's the hurry? Mom won't be home soon. That's what she was calling to tell me. Some emergency at the hospital. She's a dermatologist, for God's sake. How big of an emergency could it be?"

She put her hand behind my head and pulled me toward her, and we kissed until I would have done anything she told me. Then she said I did have to go, and so I ran back to the motel and picked up my ball and glove and kept going and ran out to the old house and repeated my performance of the day before. I threw and threw and lost and lost and then lay down in the grass, imagining her with me there, feeling her there with me.

20

We were sitting in Stroud's back room drinking iced tea. Miss Young was there again, and she and Stroud had been arguing, but he wasn't putting on an act this time. He was just talking the way he usually did. I tried to change the subject—they'd been arguing about somebody they used to know—by asking Stroud if he thought I could be a really good pitcher. He said I probably could, but that I was trying too hard.

I said I didn't know that was possible. I said I thought you were supposed to give it everything you had.

"Yeah," Stroud said, "but it's tricky."

I was sitting on the sofa beside Miss Young, and Stroud sat in the rocking chair, slowly moving up and back, pushing off with his right foot.

"You're absolutely right, Lewis." Miss Young put her hand on my forearm, patted it twice, then recrossed her arms.

Stroud stopped rocking and glared at Miss Young, his chin thrust forward. "What you know about it, old woman?" He turned to me. "See? Here she goes. Don't know a baseball from a road apple, and now she's talking about how to throw a baseball. You see how it is? Good God Almighty."

Miss Young patted the air. "Calm down now, Uncle Truman. Watch your blood pressure."

"Now she's a doctor," Stroud said. "Put her in a airplane, she'll be wrestling that walker up the aisle, yelling at the pilot what button to push."

"I do not yell, Uncle Truman. All I said was . . ."

"I know what you said. But we talking about *baseball*, woman. You got that? You might be right about *some* things, but everything ain't like everything else."

"Well, I'm not sure I know what *that* means."

Stroud turned back to me, shaking his head. "Look here. Don't pay no attention to her. It's like this, you see. You got to do two things at the same time. Got to try as hard as you can without trying so hard you beat yourself."

I asked him how you could try *too* hard if you're supposed to try as hard as you can.

"Well," he said, "like I said, before I was so crudely interrupted, it's tricky. Hard to explain to somebody that ain't ever done it." He jerked his thumb toward Miss Young. "But you got to try as hard as you can, and pull back at the same time. It's like this: if the game means too *much* to you, see, you'll mess it up nearly every time. But still and all, don't even go out there if you ain't going to give it everything you got. See what I mean?"

"It's what we call a paradox," Miss Young said.

"A pair of what?" Stroud asked.

"A paradox." Miss Young pronounced the word slowly. "An apparent contradiction that . . ."

But Stroud interrupted her with a laugh and a hard slap against the arm of his chair, and he reached out a hand to me, as if he wanted me to take it or touch it, and when I didn't, he jabbed his knuckle into my knee. "Got her *that* time," he said. "Pair of what. See what I mean? She thinks I don't know nothing. Any word longer than "dog" or "cat," she thinks she got to explain it."

Miss Young regarded him calmly.

"Oh, yeah, she going to explain it big time," Stroud said, "you can count on that. Put your last money on it. But look here. Whatever you call it—what I told you—you remember that. It's the truth."

"What's a road apple?" I said.

21

Stroud told me that when Satchel Paige was in Sabbath Creek, he did a lot of running, trying to keep in shape, even the second time he was there, when his arm was dead.

"He sure looked pitiful, though, I tell you. Tried not to move his right arm, you see. It just hung off him like a sleeve. He'd run with his hand in his pocket, so the arm wouldn't swing."

"Where did he run?"

"Pretty much the same as you, as I remember it. He'd take a left out of the motel and go down a ways, then take a right, out past the Stiles place, the house you been throwing your ball against. Same place where you done taped up that giant strike zone. One time, on his way back, he stopped there and asked the Stiles for some water, and him and old Ab Stiles got to talking, and later on, he went down there and Ab's little fat wife cooked for him. She talked with Ramona, and Ramona told her what Leroy could eat, and then she fixed it so his stomach could take it. They ate supper, and then they had a prayer meeting. Ab, he was a part-time preacher, you see, but he never did push it on anybody, and so you could stand to be around him."

"Was Satchel Paige a religious man?"

"Was *then*, when his arm was dead. I saw him a few years later, and it seemed to have worn off, but by then his arm had come back to life, and he was making big money, driving a fancy car. But when his arm was dead, he tried everything. He even went down to the rootworker, out the old Jacksonville Road—woman everybody called the fox lady. They said she used the bones and teeth of a fox in all that hoodoo she did."

"Did anything help?"

"Not while he was here. Later on, it seemed like his arm just got better, sort of gradual-like. And then finally, he got back to where he was before."

"What did you talk about while he was here? Did he tell lots of baseball stories?"

"He did the first time he was here. But the second time, when his arm was dead, he wouldn't talk about baseball. He'd get right peeved if you brought it up. One thing I do remember us talking about was the little notebook he kept. He used to write down some of the laws he ran into as a black man while traveling around the country. What they used to call the Jim Crow laws. Had them all over the place. You know what I'm talking about?"

I said I did, but he looked at me like he didn't believe me.

There was a knock on the back door, and I got up to answer it, but Stroud waved his hand for me to sit down.

"Wait a minute," he said. The visitor knocked again, louder and longer.

"Why don't you want me to open the door?"

"You want to open the door?" he said. "Go open it then."

Just as I stood up, I heard, "Uncle Truman?"

"She'll be in here in a minute," Stroud said. "Ain't no need to say nothing. She'll ask herself in. Always does."

I remembered how slowly Miss Young moved, and also how, when I met her, we'd stood outside for a long time, waiting for him to answer, so I got up and opened the door and held it for her so she could maneuver her walker through. She thanked me and moved carefully through the kitchen and into the room where Stroud sat.

"You late," he yelled out, while she was still making her way across the kitchen linoleum. She didn't answer him. She had her eyes fixed on the next place she was about to step. As she came into the room, he repeated, "You late. Twenty minutes late."

She still didn't answer. When she reached the rocker, she turned and backed toward the chair, then dropped down into it. She sat down hard, and her dress slipped up above her knees, and she quickly pulled it down, then slid back in the chair.

I told her Stroud had been talking about the book Satchel Paige had written on the old Jim Crow laws.

"I didn't say it was a book he wrote. He kept a little notebook, that's all, and he wrote in it everywhere he went — and he traveled all over the country back then, you see, and so he saw more of it than most black folk — everywhere he went, he wrote down different laws he came across, that's all. I don't believe he ever did anything with it, though. If he did, I didn't hear about it."

"You know, I recall Ramona telling me about that notebook," Miss Young said.

I asked Stroud if he could remember what was in it, and he said he did remember a few things, but that he didn't like to think about it much.

"Anyhow," he said, "don't me or her either one" — he nodded at Miss Young — "need a book to tell us how it was. We lived it every day. We could write our *own* book."

"In your case," Miss Young said, "I suggest you *read* a book before you try writing one."

"There she go," Stroud said. "Read a book. Maybe if she'd ever took something into the bedroom be*sides* a book, somebody could stand to be in the same room with her. Read a *book*."

I asked them not to start fighting, and Stroud said, "Was I fighting? I was going along talking, and she jumped me. I wasn't fighting."

Miss Young smiled at me. "I couldn't resist," she said. "What Uncle Truman said initially is correct, of course. No black person of a certain age needs a book to tell him or her about the injustices of segregation. That's the sad truth."

"But Jo," Stroud said — it was the only time I'd heard him call her by her first name — "you know he had some *real* foolishness in that notebook. I forget what state it was a law in, but say a white man and a black man was fishing in the same boat, just the two of them. If noontime rolled around, and they pulled out the sandwiches, by state law they had to lay one of the fishing poles crossways across the boat to separate the front from the back. Otherwise, they'd be eating in the same place, and they'd be breaking the law."

Miss Young said, "Oh, it was wholesale ignorance."

"And here's another one," Stroud said, "here's another one. There was courtrooms that had one bible for white folks to swear to tell the truth on, and another bible for black folk. The white bible and the black bible. Said a light-skinned man swore on the wrong bible one time, and the judge almost had a stroke, and then he held the witness in contempt of court and put him in jail."

Miss Young said, "Oh, yes, that practice of separate bibles was very common."

"Leroy had whole lists of laws about who you couldn't marry.

Just about every state he went to, and not just in the south, had laws like that. I don't even want to get started on that."

"Please don't," Miss Young said.

Stroud and Miss Young both sat there looking at the floor.

"Miss Young, here," — suddenly Stroud was speaking in a voice I had never heard; it groaned up from his chest and thickened. "She lost a first cousin up at Yellow Shoals, back in the days when white folks could do anything they wanted to a black person. Isaiah was a fine young man . . ."

"Yes, he was, goodness. Isaiah Cutts."

"And a pack of white men grabbed him and stripped his clothes off and whipped him and then blew the top of his head off with a shotgun. For nothing. Not a thing."

"He had done nothing at all, Lewis, but that didn't matter, not back then."

"What happened to the men who killed him?" I asked.

"What *happened?*" Stroud said. "Didn't *nothing* happen. That's the way it was. White men went on with their lives, died and went to heaven, for all I know."

22

Stroud said that when Satchel Paige visited the fox lady, she told him his arm was dead "because somebody had throwed against him and hexed him. Probably one of his women, she said. I don't know exactly what she did to take the spell off, but it didn't help him. That's when he got religion. He tried all that hoodoo business first, and when that didn't help, he got saved. They laid hands on him down at Ab's house. The next day, he said his arm was almost well. He walked around the motel singing and carrying on, and that night he went back to Ab's place and they laid hands on him again, and then they did it one more night, and by the time Leroy left here a few days later, he could raise his arm over his head, something he hadn't been able to do in a long time. He still couldn't pitch, though, and he wrote us a letter a week later and said his arm was worse than ever."

I asked Stroud if he and Satchel Paige were good friends.

"I wouldn't say that, no. I think he liked us, me and Ramona. We took good care of him. Sometimes he acted like he knew he was a big star. Mostly the first time he was here, though. The second time, when he was trying to get healed, he acted pretty much like everybody else. That's when I got to liking him as a man. He was a fine man, he really was, not just a ballplayer."

I asked Miss Young if she met him, and she said she not only met him, but they went out on a date. This was on his first visit to town. She was nineteen and had just finished her freshman year at Fort Valley State Normal and Industrial School. She said they went to a dance club down on the highway, and she said Satchel Paige was the wildest dancer she ever saw. She couldn't keep up with him. Other people cleared the floor at one point to watch him and some woman dance the Lindy Hop. She said she never saw a man enjoy dancing the way he did. I asked her if she fell in love with him.

"Goodness no. We merely went out dancing that one time. I'm afraid I wasn't what he was looking for, and he wasn't exactly my idea of an ideal man either."

"Huh," Stroud said. "Who *was?* Jesus Christ maybe, and you'd have made *him* get a better job."

"There's no call for sacrilege, Uncle Truman. Satchel was a very nice man. He had good manners, and he was respectful of my wishes not to become romantically involved. We spent that one evening together. We had dinner and went dancing, and he brought me home, and that was it."

"What did you talk about?" I asked.

"I need me a cigarette," Stroud said, shooting a look at Miss Young. "We keep on sitting around, we'll be late." He got up and walked out onto the patio.

I asked her where they were going, and she said she was driving him to see his doctor for a checkup. I was tempted to asked her if it was a psychiatrist they were going to see, but I didn't. "Is there something wrong with him?"

"Yes, there is," she said. "He's ninety-three years old. Other than that, he's healthier than he has any right to be. Smoking cigarettes one after the other. Lacing his food with pepper sauce too hot for Beelzebub. And he'll eat anything. I've seen him fry a pound of bacon just for himself. He'll even burn it a little, since he likes it that way."

I asked her again what she talked about with Satchel Paige.

"Oh, it's hard to remember now. He primarily asked questions about me. He didn't talk about himself much, and that was part of his charm. Some men, even those who haven't really done anything outstanding, are convinced that a woman will be interested in hearing them go on and on about themselves. And women generally go along with the charade, smiling and gazing into the man's eyes and secretly being bored. So it's often a surprise when a man expresses a genuine interest in something about the woman other than her physical attributes. But Satchel seemed to be truly interested in me. He wanted to know what Fort Valley was like, what courses I'd taken, how hard they were. I told him I'd taken a year of French, and he asked me to speak a sentence or two for him. I didn't want to, but he insisted, and when I did, I remember how delighted he was. He was a generous, sensitive man."

The back door slammed. "All right. Time to go. Take us a half hour just to get you to the car. Why don't you just go ahead and get you a wheelchair? Then we could roll you out there and be done with it."

"In vivid contrast with *some* people."

Miss Young slid forward in her chair and began struggling to stand. I helped her up, and we moved slowly toward the car, where Stroud sat in the front seat, waiting.

23

I didn't know it then, but my mother would walk out behind
the motel and follow a path that cut across the railroad tracks
and sloped downward sharply and after half a mile came to the
edge of a gully.

She would climb down and practice firing the pistol, shooting
at stumps and dead limbs and aiming at shadows on the gully
walls.

* * *

I dragged the Gideon from under the bed, but its spine broke,
and pages fell out and scattered everywhere. I picked up one of
them and read:

Be still, and know that I am God.

I found a plastic grocery bag, and I gathered the pages and
stuffed them in, then twisted the bag and tied it in a knot, and
I went out and made my way to the trashpile, and I threw the
bag onto the garbage and left it there.

24

We walked beside the pond, skipping stones and talking, and Eva wondered if the dogs ever thought about her, and if they did, what that was like for them. Did they remember her voice and her smell? Were they sad when they thought of her, and if so, did they *know* they were sad?

I told her my dog had been run over when I was eight years old, and that I'd wondered whether he knew he was dying.

"I doubt it," she said. "Maybe. But do people even know that?"

"Watch this," I said. I picked up a flat rock, went through my complete windup, and I threw the rock low and hard out over the pond, and it sank with the sound of a half-gulp, barely moving the water. Eva thought that was really funny, funnier than I thought it actually was, and I started looking for another good rock.

On the far side of the pond, several ducks had entered the water and begun swimming toward us.

"What about those ducks?" she said. "Do they even know they're ducks?"

"Of course they know they're ducks," I said. I felt a little hurt that she'd laughed so hard. "What else are they going to think they are?"

She picked up a rock, slung it sidearm over the pond, and it curved and dropped and skipped three times.

* * *

Eva's mother wanted her to be a doctor, a dermatologist, so they could practice together, but Eva said it wasn't going to happen. She couldn't stand the thought of looking at bad skin all day.

"And it's not just kids with acne," she said. She led me into her mother's study and showed me a book with photos of sickening skin conditions.

"If she thinks I'm going to be a doctor, of any kind," Eva said, "she's in for a big disappointment. I've got other plans."

She led me into another room, where there were hangings on the walls and shelves filled with small carvings and odd-looking pots. One shelf was lined with different kinds of masks, and she took one of those and put it on. It made her face look like a grinning skull, but I could see her eyes through the eyeholes.

"My mom got this in New Guinea," she said. "She's traveled all over the world."

I made her take off the mask. I didn't really want to be talking to the skull. She took down another mask, the worst-looking one of all, then led me to a mirror, handed me the mask, and told me to put it on. I didn't want to, but I did.

"I can't remember exactly where Mom bought this one," she said, "but I know it was somewhere in South America. It's a mask for driving out demons. It's supposed to be so ugly that it scares them off. The person who's possessed puts on the mask and then looks at his reflection, and it scares the demons out of his body. That's why it stinks, too, so the demons won't be able to stand it."

I put the mask on, then immediately took it off and started sneezing. It not only smelled rotten, but there was some kind of pepper or hot spice inside it. I kept sneezing, and I felt like I couldn't breathe.

Eva took the mask from my hands. "You're *supposed* to sneeze. It helps get rid of the demons," she said. "Did you get a good look at yourself?"

25

Stroud said he didn't want a funeral. He wanted to be cremated and have that be the end of it. I didn't know why he was talking about dying, and I didn't know what to say. I asked him what he wanted done with his ashes.

"Now why would I care about that?"

We were sitting out back on the patio, and he was smoking. He scowled at me, the cigarette in his mouth.

"What about your wife and your son?" I asked him. "Were they cremated?"

He'd been slouching down in his chair, and now he pulled himself up and took a deep drag off his cigarette. "No," he said, "I buried them out at the cemetery." He looked straight at me, then pointed toward the trashpile on the other side of the motel's backyard. "You see all that mess? Where you think it came from?"

I figured it was trash from the motel, but I didn't want to say that. After all, I'd found his old hat out there, so some of it must have been his, but he was such a clean old man — always scrubbing and disinfecting his apartment — it seemed odd that he'd dump trash out behind where he lived.

"If you don't want to talk about your wife and son," I told him, "I can understand that. I was just wondering, since you were talking about being cremated."

"Look here," he said, "I asked you a question."

"I guess it came from the motel. I don't know. Where *did* it come from?"

He leaned forward. "Came from the motel, that's right, some of it, after part of it burned and we tore some of it down. We hauled things out and left them there all piled up and never moved them. That's true. But some of it was old things that belonged to me and Ramona and the boy. When Tru died, Ramona held onto everything, you see. Didn't throw nothing away. And then when she died, I sort of lost my mind. I couldn't even go back in the apartment. Slept out in one of the rooms for a long time. I couldn't stand to look at her things or at Tru's things that she'd kept. And then one day I went in there and drug out everything that reminded me of her and him—well, not everything, but most everything—and I threw them out there. All Ramona's dresses and clothes and so forth, they all out there. All of Tru's things. Letters he wrote home. The mattress me and Ramona slept on. It's all been out there in the rain and sun a long time. I couldn't bring myself to keep the stuff, you see, but I couldn't throw it away either. So I guess I threw it away and kept it both. It's out there, but it's ruined and gone."

I asked him if he ever regretted throwing those things away.

"Look here," he said. "What's done is done."

He stubbed out his cigarette. I was sorry I'd asked him, and I told him that, and he said, "Well," and we sat there not talking.

26

I was standing next to one of the coolers at Furlow's, trying to decide what kind of ice-cream bar to buy, when I looked up and saw a man standing at the counter, holding out a paper bag. I couldn't see his face, but his head was mostly bald, and the little hair he had left was stubble. He was a big man — maybe six-six, probably two-fifty. He wore a T-shirt with the arms cut out, brown pants that did not reach his ankles, and heavy work shoes.

The girl behind the counter shouted, "How many you got in here?" She took the bag and dumped out the contents and counted. "Twenty, it looks like. So that's ten dollars, right? Ten dollars?"

The man didn't answer, just stood there. The girl opened the cash register and handed him a bill. He gave two sharp nods of his head, then turned abruptly and walked straight down the aisle toward me. I took a step back, and the girl said, "Don't worry, he won't hurt you."

I stared down into the cooler, and the man came and stood right beside me, slid open the cooler's top, reached in and pulled out a single ice-cream bar, the same kind I'd decided on. He made a soft noise, barely audible, with every breath he let go, almost an *oh* sound, but not quite, like the beginning of a groan cut short.

Parts of his face looked rubbery and slick. There was an oblong sunken spot, like the imprint of a tablespoon, a few inches above where his left ear should have been, where now there was a hole much larger than an ear canal, a grape-sized knot of melted skin just behind it. A raised purple scar ran from his left eyebrow backwards to the sunken spot. The right side of his mouth opened in a sneer, and the lips on the left side of his mouth seemed fused together. His right eye looked normal, but the left was a puckered socket.

I saw all this when he turned and looked directly at me and paused before walking back to the counter. He paid for the ice cream, and the girl shouted the amount of his change at him and told him to come back. The man did not react to anything she said. I watched him walk off in the opposite direction from the motel.

The girl picked up one of the carved figures she'd dumped out of the bag. "More dang fish. Every one of them. That's the way it's getting to be, all the time. Why don't he do more little dogs and stuff?"

I put my ice-cream bar on the counter and handed her a dollar.

She said, "Sort of scared you, didn't he?"

I nodded.

"It happens to everybody the first time they see him. But he won't hurt you. He's real nice, just retarded. Don't you remember me telling you that before?"

I went out, walked around to the side of the store, sat down and leaned against the wall and ate, but my throat seemed to be closing up on me.

Stroud knew about the man, and so did Miss Young. "I knew his mother," she said. "Myrtle McGrath."

Stroud said it was a shame. "Folks laugh at him, treat him like he ain't got good sense. It's true he can't talk or understand what you say to him, but he knows things. He does. Folks treat him like a dog, *worse* than a dog."

Stroud squinted at me, gave his head a little sideways dip. "You didn't hurt his feelings, did you? Act like you was scared of him?"

"No sir," I said, and I hoped I was telling the truth.

"Folks that got no business talking," Stroud said, "some of the same ones that treat him that way. Folks that was sitting on their ass while that boy was fighting a war that left him looking like he does. I don't care *where* the war was or *what* it was about. They ought to treat the boy right, that's what I say."

"Myrtle took care of him as well as she could," Miss Young said. "She's been gone almost fifteen years, and now there's no one to look after him. He's in and out of the veterans' hospitals, I understand."

Stroud said, "He can't talk or read or write anymore, after what happened to him, or understand a word you say. It's pitiful. But he still knows things. He does."

Eva told me she kept a secret notebook for recording her dreams. She dreamed often of flying—not in an airplane, but under her own power. She'd fly to Miami, where her real father lived with his other family. She'd fly through the rooms; she'd land on the dinner table and eat from the plate of her stepsister. Once, she woke up to the sound of the birds outside her window and she thought, for a dreamy second or two, that she understood what they were saying.

I told her about my dreams of my father.

She told me about her dreams of being lost in the woods and seeing a clearing and heading for it, only to have the clearing close up before she got there.

I told her about my dreams of being back in my room at home.

She told me that sometimes she laughed in her dreams, but she usually couldn't remember what was so funny.

And then I told her about being worried that I would become one of those people who have no control over their lives, like the man who had to whistle a tune and walk backwards every time he saw a cat.

28

There was a knock on the door, and when I opened it, Stroud said, "Telephone for your mama." I told him she wasn't there, and he said, "Well, *you* come talk to the man then. He's calling from over at Coleman's."

He led me through the back door of the office and into his apartment. He'd been cleaning again — I smelled ammonia and disinfectant — and he pointed toward the phone.

"I'll be in the kitchen. Don't let the man sell you nothing."

I recognized the voice of the mechanic I'd talked to the last time I was at Coleman's. He said our car was ready, and we could pick it up anytime. I hung up and told Stroud what he'd said.

"Pick it *up?* They need to deliver it *here.* You get back on the phone and tell them that. Tell them bring it on out here."

I called back, and the man told me they were pretty busy but he'd do what he could, and it was maybe two hours later when our car rolled up, followed by a wrecker. My mother was back by then. The man gave her a bill, and she studied it and asked him some questions, then reached into her purse and pulled out a roll of cash. She counted out the bills and handed them to the man, who counted them again. Just then, Stroud came out of the office.

"You done paid him?"

My mother nodded, and Stroud said, "Well, it's your money."

He walked over to the car and bent down to look at the tires. He reached inside and pulled the lever that popped the hood, then raised it and propped it open.

"Ain't no telling what they did to it. What's the paper say?"

She showed it to him, and Stroud looked at it and then at the mechanic. "Timing belt? Took y'all this long to get these folks a timing belt?"

The man just shrugged. "You know how it is."

"Oh, I *know* how it *is*. The boy told me y'all had the car up on blocks. Said you gave away the tires. Where'd you get these tires here?"

The man said, "They're good tires."

I walked around the car and looked at the tires. They seemed new. Stroud said, "Are they retreads? I think they retreads, that's what I think."

"Brand new. Shipment just came in this morning."

"*Ship*ment? That what you call it?" Stroud turned to Mom and me. "Most likely stolen, you see. Wouldn't be the first time. But I guess you take what you can get."

He went back into the office and shut the door. The man climbed into the wrecker, and when it pulled out of the parking lot, he and the driver were both laughing.

My mother said, "I should have taken it for a test drive." She got in and drove down the road a quarter mile or so, then came back. She said it seemed to be running all right, and she told me to go in and get packed, and I told her that I wasn't going anywhere.

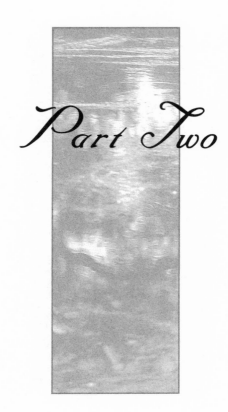

Part Two

Nearly two months earlier, my mother showed up at the ball field, called me over and made me get in the car and wouldn't explain. She floored the accelerator, and the tires shot sand and rocks back against the fence, where the other boys stood watching. She turned south onto the highway, passed a truck on the double yellow lines, took the next right, and the black-top dipped and hooked, and we flew into shadows and over a bridge, and the creek flashed beneath us, and I got that thick feeling that fills your throat when you're about to cry.

She said my father had hit her with his fist. She slowed down and turned toward me, and the left side of her face had puffed up—the white of her eye swollen, a film over the dark iris, a scrape on her cheekbone.

Somehow, I hadn't even noticed.

I can't explain it.

We drove for a few hours, and we took a room that evening at a small motel with a portable sign out front that read "Jesus is Coming Back HBO." My mother went to sleep, but I lay there awake, and it didn't help that the people in the next room never turned off the TV. I heard canned laughter and loud commercials all night, and when I did go to sleep, I dreamed about my father. His head was like a drawing in a comic strip—swollen and lopsided and topped with a tiny baseball cap. He drove on the wrong side of the road, and we ended up running on the beach, an old dog splashing along beside us through the foam.

And then my father stood still, and his giant head began to wobble and sway like it was about to fall. I dropped to my knees in the sand and got ready to catch it. I heard laughter. The old dog growled and lunged at the waves, and far out over the ocean a streak of lightning came down and froze like light in a cracked windowpane, and I got up and walked out into the water—I couldn't help it—and when I looked back, I was alone.

* * *

We drove the back roads, past cafes and motels and stores burnt out and fallen in and grown over with kudzu, past buckled slabs of concrete strewn with broken glass, weeds coming up through the cracks. We saw faded signs and billboards for roadside attractions, nearly all of them out of business now.

We stopped at a place called Pharaoh's House of Curiosity. The owner let us use the bathroom, but he told my mother that we'd have to pay ten dollars to see any of the exhibits. She paid it, and we went into a dim back room where we saw two folding tables, each lined with gallon jars. The first jar contained a baby pig floating in a cloudy fluid. It had a regular head and then half of another one—one eye, half a nose, half a mouth. The middle edge of the half-head was lined with fuzzy green spots like bread mold. All three eyes were open, but the extra eye squinted, as if the pig were trying to wink. There was a normal pig fetus in the next jar.

I started toward the second display, stumbled over my own feet and bumped the table hard, and the normal fetus twisted to its left, raised up slightly, then settled and lay still, the flakes of pale trash I'd sloshed up from the bottom of the jar drifting down.

My mother grabbed my arm and pulled me out the door. "I don't know what I was thinking," she said, and we got in the car, and she sped away. She made me turn off the radio.

* * *

I woke up, and my mother wasn't there, and I went out looking for her. We were staying in a motel next to a Dairy Queen, and I thought maybe she'd gone over there to get something to eat, but when I looked inside, I saw that it was closed. The sign was still lit up, but while I was out walking around, I saw them turn it off. There was nothing else within walking distance, just pines and the road, the motel and the Dairy Queen. I went back to the motel and walked around it, looked through the opening in the curtains of one room and saw a fat man lying naked on the bed, a pack of Oreos on his stomach, and so I went back to the room and waited. Maybe ten minutes later, she came in, leaned down, and hugged me, and her hair smelled like smoke.

The next afternoon, we rolled into another small town and stopped at a convenience store. She told me to stay in the car while she pumped the gas and went inside to pay. Two boys, both about eighteen, stood propped against the soft-drink machines beside the door, and they watched her walk past. After she was inside they looked at each other and snorted, and I heard one of them say, "Goddamn, baby." When she came out, one of the boys said, "I got what you need," but my mother kept walking.

We drove on through town, and she asked me which way I wanted to go. I kept the road map under my seat, and I pulled it out, but it was just a Georgia map.

"How much money do we have?" I asked her.

"Don't you worry about that," she said. "I told you before. Money's not our problem."

"Well, what exactly *is* our problem then?"

She gave a little hissing laugh. "Lewis," she said, "you are your father's child."

* * *

My father came looking for us.

My mother liked stopping at roadside stores, looking at old furniture and clothes, and especially old newspapers. She bought a cabinet at a store near Jesup, paid cash, and gave the salesman our address in Cofield. She told him she wanted it delivered, but not yet; she'd call him.

We drove to Savannah and spent three days there. We ate in restaurants, not barbecue shacks or convenience stores. I ate so much fried shrimp the first night, I was sick. We drove down to Tybee Island and stayed at a motel on the beach, but only for one night, since my mother saw somebody she knew there, a family from Cofield on vacation.

We left Savannah the next morning, drove back the way we'd come, and we stopped at the same store for another look at her cabinet.

The man who'd sold us the piece said, "You just missed him."

"Missed who?"

"Mr. Pope. Your husband. He came by here not more than thirty minutes ago. Asked me if I had seen you again, you and your son. I told him no, but now here you are."

"Gary was *here?*"

"Within the last hour, that's right. He had a lot of questions. He was in a big hurry, wanted to know which way you drove out of here, and I told him I didn't remember, which I didn't."

The store had immediately sent a notice to our Cofield address, confirming the purchase of the cabinet.

We took the next dirt road off the highway, followed it till it hit another paved two-lane, and then we raced down that, with no idea where it led.

* * *

We drove past gourd birdhouses, a panel truck with an American flag painted on its side, a pecan grove, a stretch of mimosas. My mother saw some late-blooming day lilies she called Blue Happiness.

The land grew flatter, irrigating machines stretching out across whole fields, others like giant home sprinklers slinging water. As we drove past one of those, for just a second, I felt shrunken to the size of an insect.

We passed a pond where cows had waded down into the water as deep as they could go, so only their noses and eyes and backs showed. We drove past a small graveyard somebody had abandoned — tall weeds and broken tombstones and the rusted hull of a car parked inside the fence.

That evening, we passed a swamp with old dead trees rising up out of it. There was a full moon and a haze over the swamp, and the bare trees seemed like they were painted on the haze, which caught the moonlight and held it. We had the windows rolled down, and a gassy, half-sweet smell washed over us in the breeze.

* * *

A truck ran over a dog and kept going. The dog flopped around and then lay completely still. My mother pulled the car over, and I ran out into the road. Blood gushed from the dog's mouth, its head twisted all the way around and one side of its face completely crushed. I grabbed the collar and a hind leg, and I dragged the dog off onto the shoulder of the road, leaving a red smear on the blacktop. The collar was hard to read, but I finally made it out: 220 Julia Drive.

We'd just passed through a small community named Pine City, maybe five stores in it. My mother said we'd go back and ask about the address at one of the stores. She got in the car, and I started to pick up the dog.

My mother told me to leave him there. We'd tell the owners where he was, and they could take care of things.

We drove back to a store called Johnny's and went inside. A display case near the door held two large cheese wheels, a single bell pepper, an opened box of baking soda. My feet slipped on the gritty floor; I recognized the smell of chicken feed. At first I thought nobody was there, but then I saw a woman behind the counter, kicked back as far as she could go in a green recliner. She waved at us.

"Morning." She gave no sign that she planned to get up.

We stepped to the counter, and my mother leaned over. "How are you today?" she said. "Maybe you can help us."

The woman reached down and slung the recliner's handle forward, and the chair made a booming twang as it swung upright. She struggled to her feet and stepped to the counter.

"All right now, what can I do for you?"

She was maybe sixty years old; she smiled and her teeth looked new—white as a dinner plate and perfectly even, but a bit too large for her mouth.

"I'm Charlene Pope," my mother said, "and this is my son, Lewis. We're looking for a street called Julia Drive. Maybe you know where it is?"

"Where y'all from?" the woman asked, and my mother told her.

"My husband had a brother lived up there. Maybe you know him. Dunbar Ellison, but they called him Smiley?"

My mother told her she didn't remember the name. She asked again about the street, and the woman told us how to get there—second left, then another left. "Put you right on it," she said. "Who y'all going to see?"

"We don't really know," my mother said. "We saw an accident just a few minutes ago. A truck ran over a dog and killed it but didn't stop. We checked the collar, and it gave a Julia Drive address."

"What number?"

"220."

"220. That's Emory Starnes, I believe. What kind of dog is it? A old collie? That's what Emory's got. Old collie named Rocket. Was it a collie?"

"Yes, ma'am, it was."

The woman ran her tongue over the top row of her big teeth. "Lord," she said, "that'll kill Emory. He lives for that dog. Don't have nobody else. Got him after his wife died, when the dog was just a puppy, and he run around so fast, Emory called him Rocket. Lately, he couldn't even walk good. Not a rocket no more, that's for sure."

A car with a loud muffler pulled up and parked outside the store. For a short while that's all we could hear, and then the driver cut the engine. The woman said, "That dog's time had come though, I reckon. Even a dog has got its time. The Lord giveth and the Lord taketh away. You go out here, second left, then left."

She looked tired all of a sudden, and she sat down heavily in the recliner, and she raised a hand as we turned to walk out.

"Y'all come back."

At 220 Julia Drive we found a dark little house closed up tight, no car in the driveway, the shades pulled, and we knocked on the door, but nobody came.

My mother shouted, "Mr. Starnes?" No answer.

"Mr. Starnes, it's about your dog."

The door opened as if Mr. Starnes had been standing just on the other side of it.

"What's that now?" he said. I couldn't see him too well because I was looking at him through the rusty screen door, but I could hear him breathing hard. He didn't wait for my mother to tell him what she had to tell him. He opened the door and stepped out.

"Rocket?" He sucked back his breath and shouted it again, "Rocket, boy?"

"Mr. Starnes," my mother said, "I'm Charlene Pope, and this is my son, Lewis. We saw your dog get hit by a truck. I'm afraid he's dead. We got your address off the collar."

"Say he's dead? Well, he had no business out of the house anyhow. Couldn't half see. Deaf as a stick. Where's he at?"

"We left him by the road," she said. "We'll be glad to help you, whatever you want to do with him."

"Is he all cut up?"

"Not all that bad. No, sir."

But the dog's head was twisted around, his face crushed, teeth broken, guts spilled out. She put her hand on the old man's shoulder.

"Well, I appreciate it, I do," he said, "but I've got somebody I can call. They'll take me down there to see about him. But I appreciate it." He glanced up, as if checking the weather, and then he thanked us again and stepped back into the house and shut the door.

We found the dog just like we'd left him. We waited there a few minutes, and then a car pulled up, and Mr. Starnes got out. My mother waved, and he waved back, and I saw him step over and look down at the dog. He had another old man with him, and they both stood there looking down, and when we drove off, they still hadn't moved.

* * *

My mother had withdrawn all the money from the savings and checking accounts she shared with my father. It was not a large amount, but it left him with nothing.

The day she bought the pistol, we had walked over to the pawnshop next to the laundromat where we were washing our clothes. I was in the back of the store playing with the golf clubs when I turned and saw my mother holding a pistol in her right hand. The gun's chamber was open, and she looked down into it as the store owner reached over the counter, pointing at something on the gun.

"It's real popular," I heard him say, "and it'll do the job." She handed him the cash, and when we went back to the laundromat, my mother had a Smith & Wesson K-22 in her purse.

* * *

We must have seen a hundred misspelled signs while we were driving around, and I'm not counting the deliberate mistakes made by people trying to be cute. Some of the misspellings were merely signs with letters fallen off, but most were simple errors. "Tractor for Sell" or "Watermillions Turn Here." And my mother's favorite, "Sunday Morning Daniel in the Loins Den."

I had a dictionary that I would read sometimes while we were driving. I started looking at the short words and making a list: *cade, gleet, dorp, spall, gink, scurf*—words that I thought I should already know the meaning of.

When I was a small child, my mother and I talked to each other in a nonsense language. I'd forgotten that until she mentioned it one afternoon. I had stopped playing along when I was around five, she said.

Maybe fifty miles down the road, it came back to me: I'd stopped answering her because I'd thought she might be making sense, and that maybe I'd been making sense too, without knowing it.

And then I was looking at the dictionary one day, and I started to feel sick. Suddenly, the words seemed like a kind of mockery.

* * *

Every afternoon when he came home from work, my father and I would go out back and play ball, just the two of us. Almost always baseball, but sometimes we'd shoot baskets or throw the football, and we'd play till dark.

My mother saw how much I missed baseball, and one day she tried playing catch with me. She did better than I expected, but then a girl came out onto the balcony of the motel, and I overthrew the ball into the dirt, smoked it into the ground about four feet in front of her—she was squatting down like a catcher—and it bounced up and caught her just above the collarbone and left a bad bruise that seemed like it was never going away.

* * *

My closest friend was Andy Wilbur, the best ballplayer in Cofield. He once hit four home runs in a game, the last one a low line drive that rose like a golf shot and was still rising when it hit the oak on the other side of the fence. He only hit one homer off me, and that was when I was walking him intentionally and threw the ball over the plate by mistake.

My problem was always control. Back in Little League, a nine-year-old cried and said he didn't want to bat against me, so the coach took him out of the game, and then I hit the boy who took his place. He whirled and tried to get out of the way, but the ball caught him between his shoulder blades and made a *thunk* that you could probably hear in the outfield bleachers.

My first girlfriend was Kay Amerson. We made out in the

concession stand behind the football field, but then she wrote me love notes that misspelled easy words, and after a few of those—even as good-looking as she was—I didn't feel the same. I never told her why, though, since I didn't want to feel like that, and I didn't really understand it, and I had no control over it.

* * *

I used to worry about the size of my nose and the shape of my ears. I remember standing at the bathroom mirror, using a hand mirror too so I could study the back of my head to see whether or not it stuck out in a funny way like the head of a boy at school. I had just started the sixth grade. My head seemed all right, I thought—a little funny—but I discovered that my nose was enormous if you looked at it from the side.

Then I looked closely at the rest of my head, and I saw that my ears didn't match—my right ear had a small notch at the top and my left one didn't, and the left one looked a little bigger, too. I tried bending my ear to get the notch out, and when that didn't work, I thought of ways to put a notch in the other ear—maybe I could crimp it with a paper clip or a bobby pin—but then I realized how stupid that would be. And I couldn't do anything about my nose, either. I pressed it and pushed it, but it stayed the same, a permanent disfigurement. I looked at it over and over, as though I thought perhaps I had simply been wrong about its size, as though the next time I checked, it would be smaller, but it never was, and so I started putting a hand to my face when I talked to somebody up close.

We were attending a reunion of my mother's side of the family when I overheard the story of how Mom and Dad met. We'd already eaten, and I was heading off to play ball, but I had come back to the picnic tables for a drink, and I'd stopped and listened while I gulped down two glasses of iced tea. I sat behind a big cooler and nobody saw me, and I heard them telling stories about people getting drunk.

Mom's brother, Uncle Lewis, said, "Drunkest man I ever saw was Perry Jackson, back when we'd just got out of high school, maybe a year. The night he got so drunk, he called himself not drinking, because he was just drinking beer. He'd promised his girlfriend—I remember what she looked like, but I forget her name; who was it, Charlene?"

My mother didn't answer; maybe she shrugged, but I couldn't see her from where I was.

Uncle Lewis said, "Well, whoever it was, he'd promised her to stay sober, so he was only drinking beer. Been fishing all afternoon, drinking beer. Hadn't had a thing to eat, so by eleven o'clock that night, he was kneewalking. But he wouldn't pass out, and he wouldn't shut up. We'd all gone out to the old Radford place off the Macon highway—we were all parked out there—and then everybody'd got out and gone up on the porch. It was a full moon, and the house was way up on a hill. There was a steep bank that sloped down a good hundred yards to the highway. Anyhow, when Perry wouldn't shut up, the girl, what's her name, she shoved him, and he fell off the porch and rolled clear to the highway. Took him a long time.

He hollered the whole way down. Funniest thing I ever heard in my life."

My father said, "What did he sound like, Lewis?" I could tell he'd heard the story before.

Uncle Lewis let out a long roll of whoops and groans and screeches and snorts and howls and half-words and squealing and wheezing and yelping sounds, got everybody laughing, and when it died down, Uncle Leon, Mom's other brother, said, "But *this* family's done some drinking too, hadn't we?"

Everybody laughed again, and Mom said, "All right, y'all. That'll be enough."

"Grain alcohol, wasn't it?"

"Yes, Lewis. I'd never drunk that stuff before. I had no idea how strong it was. Billy Moon had mixed it with orange juice, and you couldn't really taste it, and I forgot it was in there."

"Dancing on a tabletop out at the VFW, with half your clothes on."

"I had *clothes* on, Lewis."

"Now, Lewis," Dad said, "her blouse was open, that's all."

I didn't want to hear any more, and I sneaked off.

* * *

My father worked for a company that made blue jeans and other denim products. He'd started out loading trucks, and the company had eventually made him the supervisor of that area. People in the office had been impressed by how well he kept his records, and a few years later when an opening came up, they offered him an entry-level bookkeeping job.

My mother worked for the weekly newspaper in Cofield. She wrote local news stories—about the school board or the county government—but she also wrote feature stories about interesting people, and she compiled and edited the information sent in by local contacts from places too small to have a post office, such as Razor's Edge, called that because the whole community was made up of a store and a few houses, all on one side of a two-lane highway. The paper's contact at Razor's Edge was a Mrs. Kirkwood, and my mother would sometimes share with us what she sent in as news: maybe the younger Willard son had spent a Saturday afternoon washing his car, or the Hattaway family had taken particular enjoyment in the fried okra one evening. Our favorite line from Mrs. Kirkwood—but one that made me feel bad for laughing—was submitted for a year-end summary article:

"Several people from Razor's Edge died last year, especially Mrs. Edna Burgess."

One afternoon when my mother and I were driving around, we came over a hill and discovered a line of cars pulled to the side of the road, their lights on. At the front of the long procession was a hearse with a flat tire, men in black suits rushing around it like a pit crew. We both laughed, and I got that Edna Burgess feeling again.

* * *

My mother stopped at a Holiday Inn off I-75, an unusual move, since she always tried to stay away from the interstate motels.

I swam in the pool, and she rubbed lotion all over herself and tried to get a tan, put a towel on the hot cement beside the pool and stretched out on it.

I decided to see how long I could swim underwater. I swam from one end of the pool to the other, counting seconds, but I could tell that the longer I stayed under, the faster I counted, so I asked my mother to time me. She'd left her watch in the room, and I offered to go get it, but she said no.

After a while, I rolled over into the dead man's float, my arms spread out, face in the water, and I held it as long as possible, then made a choking noise, my mouth just out of the water. Nothing happened. I floated harder, put everything I had into being dead, until finally I gurgled out, "Help," and my mother said, "Please, Lewis. You're drowning much too loudly."

I'd been in so many motels, I felt like an expert. There would be little bars of cheap crumbly soap; a wobbly table with a light hanging over it; a long, low chest of drawers that the TV sat on, often bolted down; a rug with a sharp odor that could make your eyes water; the whole room with a permanent smell of stale smoke and flowery air freshener, a stink that seeped into your clothes and stayed there.

At the Holiday Inn that night, I asked my mother how many people she thought had slept in our beds.

She said, "Too many people, Lewis," and she laid her book down, got up and put on her robe and sat in a chair.

But I kept on thinking about it, all those strangers who had been exactly where *I* was, stretched out right there.

* * *

My mother bought an old VCR at a junk store. Most towns had a place where you could rent videos, though it might be no more than a section in a 7-11. Some of the movies were good, and some were so bad we enjoyed them as if they were comedies, but most were just bad enough to bore us. Many of them seemed like long TV shows, but with more violence and profanity and sex. Neither of us was comfortable watching movies together when there was much sex in them, so we tried to stay away from those, but we couldn't always tell in advance. We'd fast-forward through the sex scenes, but sometimes when she left me alone in the room, I'd go back and watch them at normal speed.

She bought three used tapes for five dollars. One of these was *Tender Mercies,* a movie she'd never seen but watched over and over after we bought it. When we didn't have another movie or when there was nothing on TV, we'd watch *Tender Mercies* again, but after we'd seen it maybe eight times, my mother threw it away.

When Robert Duvall has been sober for a while, he goes out and almost starts drinking again but doesn't, and when he comes home, he smiles at his wife and says, "I'm not drunk. I bought a bottle, but I poured it all out. I'm not drunk."

There's a scene where his daughter comes to visit him. They haven't seen each other in a long time, and this is the last time he sees her alive. Her mother, a famous country singer, has forbidden her to visit him, but she's done it anyway. They talk for a short while, and right before she leaves she asks him about a song he used to sing to her when she was a little girl.

"It was something about a dove. Mama says she never heard you sing it to me."

"I don't remember that," Duvall says. "I don't."

When his daughter is gone, he stands looking out the window, and he sings the song.

At the end, he's working in the small vegetable garden out behind the motel, having just returned from his daughter's funeral. His wife is out there with him, and one of the things he says to her is, "I don't know the answer to nothing, not a blessed thing."

As he talks, the camera moves very slowly to the right, and as it does, you can see the scarecrow standing behind him — two long sticks tied together, a dress hung over the figure, a stuffed head without features and wearing a cloth cap, one arm raised, a branch stuck through the end of it, as if the scarecrow were poised to strike downward. Something bright, like a strip of tin-foil, dangles from the lowered arm, and the dress blows sideways in the breeze.

* * *

We stayed in a motel next to a field where a team of older boys was practicing. I walked over there with my glove, and the coach asked me what position I played, and then he let me throw some batting practice. He told me to throw hard, and I hit two players — one on the leg and the other on the shoulder — and most of my other pitches were too far off the plate to swing at. The players started yelling at the coach to get me out of there.

He called me over and put his arm around me, got me in a loose headlock, and we took a few steps down the first-base line. He'd been chewing tobacco, and his breath was so bad I had to turn toward left field.

"You got a good arm, son, but I don't care if you throw a hundred miles an hour. If you don't throw the ball over the plate, they don't *have* to hit you. If I was coaching a team batting against you, I'd have them take a full count before they swung. Shit, we might not *ever* swing the bat."

He squirted a wad of spit at the ground, and most of it landed on my shoe.

* * *

My mother always said you have to look for what's not obvious; you have to practice that in small ways. We'd be riding along, and she'd tell me to look around. She'd slow down, or she might stop so I could take my time.

One day, she pulled onto the side of the road just after lunch. I thought maybe the car had overheated, since it was close to a hundred degrees outside, but she didn't cut the engine.

"Look over there," she said, pointing toward a farmhouse with a barn next to it and a hilly pasture behind, where maybe twenty large black-and-white cows were lying down. We sat looking at the farmhouse for maybe ten minutes, and then after we'd gone on down the road, she asked me to tell her what I'd seen.

"There's still a Christmas wreath on the front door," I said.

We came around a curve, a car disappeared over a hill in front of us, but just before that, the driver slung a bag of trash back over the roof of the car. The bag burst apart, as though someone had shot it. Wrappers and paper cups and napkins scattered across the road, and when we reached the crest of the hill, we saw that one of the cups had landed upright, in the middle of our lane, the straw still stuck in the top.

"What are the chances of that?" Mom said. She drove straight over the cup and crushed it. I looked back and saw the flat cup and the trash swirling in our wake.

"Back there," she said, "that little lot between the house and the old milkbarn? There must be twenty years of manure in that lot, and it's right next to the house, and all the windows are open."

We drove all afternoon until we came over a hill and found traffic backed up. We could see flashing lights ahead, and as we moved closer to the accident, we saw that people had pulled their cars over and walked up to get a better look.

I thought of my father then, and I'm sure my mother thought of him too. He was a very careful driver, and whenever we were on a trip and we came across a wreck like that, he'd point out the onlookers, who really bothered him. He didn't understand how someone could use another person's trouble, maybe even tragedy, for their own amusement. When we'd pass the wreck, he would make me look straight ahead, out of respect for the people who might be injured and dying there and who didn't need others gawking and pointing at them. As far as I could tell, my mother felt the same way. If she didn't, she never said anything.

But that afternoon, without my father along, Mom and I both took a long look at the wreck. It was a single-car accident. A small red car—an old model that I didn't recognize—had evidently rolled more than once. All the car's glass was shattered or missing, the tires flat, the top crushed in, the hood and the doors like they'd been beaten with a sledgehammer.

And there was a crowd of maybe twenty people gathered near the ambulance. I saw a man in a uniform bending over a stretcher. I noticed a young man wearing headphones, and I wondered if he was listening to a CD while he watched some-body dying or dead, and I understood it a little better then, why my father felt the way he did.

After we passed the wreck, my mother sped up, and when we came to a long straightaway, she floored it. I looked over to see how fast she was going, and it was close to ninety. I told her to slow down, and she did, but I wondered why she'd drive like that, so soon after we'd seen such a bad wreck.

Just before the sun went down, we crossed a narrow bridge above a ravine that must have been a hundred feet deep. I couldn't make out what was at the bottom — whether or not it was a stream — but I didn't see any water. There were no signs on the bridge to identify it.

I had the sensation of flying as we went across the bridge. The road curved and the sky turned a different color — streaked with layers of red and gray — and then the road turned downward all at once, like a mountain road, and the sky seemed like it was beneath us somehow, for just that moment.

* * *

We ate breakfast at a small restaurant full of people, mostly men. We sat at a table near the door and the cash register, the only table left. My mother ordered coffee for herself and a full breakfast — ham, eggs, grits, and toast — for me. I asked her why she wasn't eating; she said she wasn't hungry. That was hard for me to believe, since we hadn't eaten in a long time and my stomach hurt.

Where we sat, we could hear what people said as they paid their bills. The woman working the cash register seemed to be the owner. She was older than the two waitresses, and she told them what to do, and she wasn't dressed in a uniform.

A big man wearing overalls handed her his money. "Seen old Parsons lately?"

She placed the bill in the register and counted out the man's change, her lips moving just a little. As she handed him the change, she leaned forward over the counter and said, "Let me tell you a thing or two about that joker. Come in here the other morning drunk, wanted me to serve him breakfast. I found out later that Shirley wouldn't let him back in the house. I wouldn't have let him in neither. Get this — had his shirt on inside-out. Went home like that, and Shirley pitched a Dido, and I don't blame her. I told him to come back after he sobered up."

The big man shook his head. "He ain't never going to change, is he?"

"I tell you *one* thing," the woman said. "If he was *my* husband and come home drunk with his shirt on inside-out, *I'd* change him around some. You can believe *that*."

When our food came, I picked up my fork and started to eat, but my mother made me stop while she bowed her head and said a silent grace. Sometimes she did that, sometimes she didn't. She never prayed out loud, so I don't know what she said. My eggs were not cooked the way I liked them. They were too runny. The toast was cold and spongy. The grits weren't hot either. The pat of margarine I put on top of them didn't melt. There was only raspberry jelly, which I didn't like. The little strip of ham was mostly fat. I wondered why the place was so crowded, if this was the kind of food they served, but I ate everything on my plate.

* * *

About a month before my mother and I left Cofield, someone started beating on our door at 4:30 A.M., really pounding on it.

I could hear the person shouting, over and over, "Mr. Pope, it's Woodrow Bates. Mr. Pope, it's Woodrow Bates."

I heard my father run down the hall, and I got up and put on my pants and followed him, and when he opened the door, Mr. Bates, the man who delivered our newspaper, shouted again, as though he were still trying to wake us up, "Mr. Pope, this is Woodrow Bates, your paper man."

Dad opened the door and asked him in, but he didn't move. He seemed confused. He scowled, as if the light hurt his eyes, and he repeated what he'd just said, but softer now, "This is Woodrow Bates, your paper man."

I thought that was an odd way to put it. It sounded like the sort of thing you'd say to somebody over the phone, but not to a person standing in front of you — the sort of thing you'd say to somebody who didn't know you, but we'd known him for years.

My father said, "Come on in, Mr. Bates."

Mr. Bates didn't move. "I'm broke down out here with a flat tire. I'm sorry to bother you this time of morning," he said, "but I got this arthritis in my back real bad. Doctor says I ought to be in the bed. So will you change my tire for me? I still got half my route to go."

Mr. Bates was a heavy man, seventy-three years old. His friends called him Redbone, but neither Dad nor I knew his age or his nickname until the week after he showed up at our door, when we saw his obituary in the paper.

My father hesitated, and Mr. Bates pulled out his wallet and opened it. "Be worth five dollars."

Dad told him to put his money away. He said we'd help him,

but that he needed to get some shoes on, and again he asked Mr. Bates to come inside, but the man turned and walked back toward the car.

He had already pulled the jack and lug wrench from the trunk when we got out there, and he was struggling with the heavy spare. His wife sat in the front seat, on the same side as the flat. At first I thought she was asleep, but when I came around to help my father position the jack, I saw her eyes. She nodded when I spoke to her, but then she looked straight ahead. After Dad got the jack started, he let me take over. I saw the woman's head inching upwards as I pumped the handle.

While we worked, Mr. Bates talked. He said he'd smoked for forty years but gave it up in one day. Never touched another one. He said he had a daughter in Detroit with a good job; she worked for the water system. He listed some of the jobs he'd had over the years—army cook, truck driver, school custodian, laborer.

The long green Pontiac creaked and swayed as we jacked it up. Mr. Bates said the doctor told him he had a problem with his equilibrium, and he asked me if I knew what that meant. I said, "Yes sir," but he told me anyway. When we'd finished, he thanked us over and over, and he tried to give my father the five dollars again, but Dad wouldn't take it. Then that afternoon, when he came home from work and checked the mail, Dad found a five-dollar bill in the mailbox.

When we saw Mr. Bates's obituary, I couldn't stop thinking about that morning—my father crouched over, working in the poor light; how the old man's wife sat there in silence and stared straight ahead; and how Mr. Bates talked on and on, steadying himself against the car and telling his stories, and how we might have been the last people to hear them.

* * *

After supper, my father would begin to drink. I usually went back to my room to do homework or watch television, and my mother and father would sit in the den and have a drink—the same routine every night.

One evening, after I'd been in my room for a while, I passed through the den on my way to the kitchen, and I guess I had an expression on my face that bothered him. I remember being worried about a test scheduled for the next day.

He grabbed my arm when I passed his recliner and said, "What's *your* problem?" I got the feeling they'd already been fighting when I walked in. I just shrugged and tried to go on, but he wouldn't turn me loose.

"I asked you a question."

"Nothing," I said, and I jerked my arm away and walked into the kitchen. He got up and followed me, and he leaned over and put his face close to mine.

"Don't you walk away from me while I'm talking to you. Do you understand me?"

What I did understand was this: there was no way to figure out the right thing to do when he was like that. Whatever I said, he could turn it into something bad. When he was like that, I didn't know how to stand, how to hold my face. If I looked directly at him, he might accuse me of glaring. If I looked down, he might ridicule me, tell me to hold my head up. And if I ever started to cry, as I did once or twice, that really set him off.

He'd laugh his fake laugh, screw up his face, talk to the ceiling. *God, what have I raised here?* And if I stood there and didn't do anything, if I said "yes, sir" and then waited, trying not to look or sound wrong, not to make a wrong move, then he might accuse me of acting like he was crazy, of acting like I was scared of him.

But those were also the only times — when he had been drinking — that my father ever said he loved me, the only times I ever heard him tell my mother that he loved her. He became someone else when he drank, and we never knew who would show up.

* * *

The day our car broke down, my mother had driven all night, something she'd never done before. I woke up and looked at the clock and it was 5:00 A.M., and we were still going down the road. My mother seemed wide awake; she had the radio on low, listening to a jazz station, somebody playing saxophone.

We were far out in the country, black all around us. And then we topped a small hill, and a line of lights floated on the dark field, and we rounded a curve, and a farmhouse was lit up like a prison — large bulbs on three tall poles surrounding the yard, the tin roof shining like a blade — and then all this was behind us. She'd rolled down her window, and the weed fields smelled musty, the car engine oily and hot.

"Why don't you go on back to sleep?" she said. "We'll get some breakfast in a little bit."

I did sleep, and I dreamed about my father again. This time it was really him, and his head didn't belong in a cartoon. He wore a good Sunday suit and drove an old car, and he followed us along the road, but couldn't catch us. Every time he got close, his car started to cough and slowed down. Then I was riding in the car with him instead of my mother, telling him to go faster. I looked over, and I saw that he'd taken his hands off the wheel, and he was playing the saxophone. The car stayed on the road, steering itself. There was a man in the back seat—I didn't recognize him—playing drums on a suitcase.

I asked my father when he'd learned to play the saxophone, and he said, "I can't," and then the music stopped and the car swerved off the road.

* * *

I already knew what a paradox was, long before Miss Young tried to explain it to me: a father you loved and whose love you needed so much it was like deep thirst; a father who made you sick with his drinking, made you hate him, but who tossed the ball back and forth with you for hours in the backyard, each lob or hard throw like a sentence passed between you, almost as good as words.

Part Three

1

Coleman's Auto returned our car, and I told my mother that I was not leaving Sabbath Creek. I was through driving around and staying in motels.

We argued, and then she gave up and left me alone and drove Stroud into town.

I walked around to Stroud's back door, opened it, and went inside. I looked in the refrigerator. There were three kinds of milk—regular milk, chocolate milk, and buttermilk. There was a pitcher of water and a carton of orange juice, a few sticks of butter, a package of bacon, a carton of eggs, and an unopened package of cheese. Except for the shelf of medicines and a box of baking soda, that was it. I read the labels on the medicine bottles, but the names of the drugs meant nothing to me. Most of them didn't say what they were for, though some did—he had medications for pain, dizziness, cough, nausea, and blood pressure. The rest—most of them, that is—had only the drug name and directions for taking it.

I looked through all the kitchen cabinets. I looked through his collection of hot sauces, but they didn't interest me much, except for the ones that had the drawings of sexy women on the label.

I went into his bedroom and looked through his closets and his chest of drawers, but I found nothing of any real interest. I went into the next room, the one with all the photographs on the walls, and I looked in the drawers of the desk, the drawer of the table. I pulled out the cushions of the sofa and searched under them. I went back into the bedroom and looked under the bed. I opened the closet again and started feeling inside the pockets of his clothes. I found handkerchiefs and put them back. I found an old suitcase at the bottom of the closet, but I couldn't get it open. I got a knife from the kitchen and worked at the latch until it gave way, but there was nothing in the suitcase. I went back to the chest of drawers and searched each drawer again, running my hands along the bottoms and scrambling everything up. I pulled the top drawer out and dumped it on the bed, and I knew then that everything was over for me, somehow it was all over, and when I heard the car door, I didn't even try to put things back. I just sat on the bed and waited. I looked down at the old man's underwear and I thought *what am I?*

I waited, but no one came in. I looked out the window and saw Miss Young struggling toward the apartment with her walker. I put the clothes in the drawer and put the drawer back, and by the time I'd finished, she was knocking on the door. I opened it and told her I couldn't find Stroud or my mother and that I'd come inside to look for a note, but that I hadn't found one.

She sat down in a kitchen chair, only a few steps from the door.

"Well," she said, "it looks as if I've made a trip out here for nothing. I was supposed to take him to the courthouse to deal with a tax matter. Where could he have gone?"

I told her we had our car back and that maybe my mother had taken him to the courthouse.

"It appears that way, doesn't it? He could have called me,

though, don't you think? Very inconsiderate. He doesn't realize how hard it is for me to get around, or if he does realize it, he simply doesn't care."

"Why doesn't he have his own car?" I asked her. "He's got great eyesight and great reflexes for a man his age. Nobody would believe it. He can catch everything I throw to him."

"Oh, I know it. He lost his license years ago, for speeding, and since then he has simply refused to apply for another one. He's a stubborn old man. He doesn't like people asking him questions and giving him tests. You should have seen him when he was in the hospital. He was a terror."

"Why was he in there?"

She said he had collapsed out in front of the motel one afternoon. Someone driving by had seen it happen and called an ambulance. The doctors found nothing seriously wrong with him, but they kept him in the hospital overnight for observation. While he was there, he coughed up blood, so they did X rays and ran tests and kept him for two more nights. Then he caught some kind of infection, and they had a hard time treating it, and he ended up staying there for two weeks.

Miss Young said, "He claims that he did not collapse but that he tripped and hit his head and briefly lost consciousness. He says the hospital almost killed him, and he vows never to enter another one. I'm sure nursing staffs everywhere are hopeful that he keeps his promise."

She said she wasn't going to wait around for him, and she stood and slowly made her way to the door, down the steps, and to her car. I walked with her, trying to help, and when she was gone, I went back into the apartment and tried to make things look as though nobody had been there.

* * *

My mother drove Stroud to the grocery store the next morning, and I went along.

On the way back, she stopped at an estate sale. I was surprised to see a price tag on what looked like an old family picture, framed and sitting beside the woman's bed. I thought maybe the son was just selling the frame, but he said he was selling the photo too, if anybody was willing to buy it. He said it was a picture of his mother and father.

We bought nothing, got back in the car, and headed to the motel. My mother drove, and Stroud gave directions, just as he had done earlier.

"Turn up here. Slow down. Keep your eyes on the road. Light's green. Speed up a little. Watch that hole. Put both hands on the wheel."

Miss Young had once said that driving Stroud around Sabbath Creek had brought her "as close to actual physical assault on another person as I have ever come." I thought about that now, but my mother paid him little attention.

We were almost back at the motel when she said to him in a low voice, "So, as far as what we were talking about, that's the way I feel."

Stroud nodded.

"Feel like what?" I asked her.

"Nothing, Lewis. We were just talking." But I could tell. It was something.

2

I woke up, and my mother was gone again. I went out to look for her, and I noticed there was a light in Stroud's apartment. I sneaked up close to a window, and looking through a crack in the curtains, I saw them sitting in the room with all the photos on the walls.

My mother was crying. Stroud was sitting in the chair opposite her. I saw his lips move, but I couldn't hear what he was saying. I went around to the office entrance and tried the door. It opened, and I went in and moved quietly toward the thin line of light that came through the slightly opened door connecting the office and Stroud's apartment.

I put my ear to the opening, and I heard my mother say, "But it was. I know that now. It was all a mistake, the whole thing."

"What's that?" Stroud asked.

"Everything."

I put my eye to the crack in the door, and I saw my mother sitting with her face buried in her hands. Stroud sat back in his chair, legs crossed, and he was smoking a cigarette, which was unusual since he didn't usually smoke inside his apartment.

"Even Lewis," she said. "I love him more than anything in the world, but he was a mistake too."

"Now, hold it right there," Stroud said. "You just hold it. That right there is the worst kind of foolishness, and you know it is.

That boy ain't no mistake. He's your precious gift. I *lost* my boy, and I *know*. That boy ain't no mistake. He's the best thing ever happened to you. You know that. I don't want to hear nothing about a mistake."

My mother blew her nose on a tissue. "Oh, I know it, and I would die if anything ever happened to him. And that's not just an expression, either—I don't think I would survive. I didn't mean he was really a mistake. He's my baby. But you don't know the whole story."

Crouching in that dark room, looking through a crack in the door, I felt like I was in a movie theater and also in a movie.

"I never wanted to be anybody's wife," she said, "and I *never* wanted to be anybody's mother. I had just come back home for a little while after college. That's what I thought, anyhow. I was going to save some money and travel. I was going to see other parts of the world. I thought maybe I'd get married at some point, but I *never* wanted children. When I found out I was pregnant, I made an appointment to get rid of it, but Gary talked me out of doing that."

Get rid of *it*.

"You lucky he did," Stroud said. "You know that. You got a fine boy."

"But I hate my life," my mother said. "I really do."

I pulled away from the door as quietly as I could. I heard Stroud say, "No, you don't."

I eased out of the office, went back to the room and got some money from my mother's purse, then went out to the highway and started running, and as I ran, I kept hearing her say the words *get rid of it,* and I started saying them under my breath, and then they locked onto the rhythm of my steps, and some of the words fell away, until finally I was saying that one word, *it*, over and over, every time my left foot hit the ground.

I remembered the pictures I'd seen one day when I went to a college football game with my father. Just outside the stadium, there was a platform where people could give speeches, and one young man was shouting and holding up large posters with photos of bloody, twisted fetuses. He pointed out the little ears, hands, eyes. He pointed out how the mouth seemed to be open in a scream.

I ran hard. I followed the highway through town, and then I was on a road I'd never seen before. About a mile outside of Sabbath Creek, the road forked, and I went to the right. I ran past a white frame church with a large graveyard beside it. The moon hung low over the pines behind the graveyard, and a light set under the eaves of the church cast a glow over the stones close by. The moonlight caught a strand of fencewire that flickered once and went dark.

I felt the road change under my feet. The pavement stopped, and I was running on dirt. Trees rose higher on both sides. I ran down a steep hill, almost losing my balance. The air felt cooler, and it smelled different now — strong and rich and with an edge, like pinestraw after rain — and then I heard a rasping, and it grew louder. The road turned and flattened out, and I could see it — the creek and the rocks flashing darkly under the moon.

I stopped running. I walked onto the narrow bridge and stood looking at the water, then crossed over, crawled down the bank, and came up under the bridge. I sat on the cool clay that sloped toward the water, and then I lay back. My blood beat in my ears for a while, then got quieter; my fast breath slowed down. The rush of water made the same hushing and hissing sounds over and over, as though they had gone on forever and would never stop. I lay there and looked up at the blank underside of the bridge, and after a while I felt my hands unclench themselves.

* * *

I awoke knowing I had dreamed something bad, but it would not come back to me, and then I remembered the night before, remembered where I was. My mother's words rushed into my arms and legs, shot down into my stomach, and I sat up.

I walked down to the creek and washed my face. The water was cool and felt good, but I knew not to drink it. I looked upstream and saw a clearing on the bank, a small sandbar, and a rope hanging from a limb that stretched out over the creek. I walked back up the bank and found a narrow path that led to the clearing. Someone had built a fire there in the last few days. There was a wire trashcan half filled with paper and bottles. Near the top, I found a box full of gnawed chicken bones; it held two biscuits that appeared untouched. I smelled them, inspected them closely, then ate them. They tasted gummy and dry. I looked around for an unopened can or bottle, but found nothing I wanted to risk. I'd had no water after my long run of the night before, and now the biscuits made me desperate for something to drink. It would have to be the creekwater, even though I remembered what Stroud had told me—it was polluted with waste from the chicken processing plant upstream. But when I kneeled down to draw the brown water to my mouth, I saw movement on my left. A strip of plastic hung from a bush, and two cans bobbed and shifted under the water. I reached over and pulled out two tall Budweisers.

The first gulp was bitter and awful, but the next few were not as bad. I was so thirsty I drained the whole can and opened the other one. I slid back up the bank and leaned against a tree. Directly in front of me, far out over the creek, a rope hung down from a branch. The rope fell about a foot short of the water, and as it hung there not moving, it seemed to move. The water flowed past, and the rope, as I fixed my eyes on it, seemed to slip sideways upstream. I held my eyes steady on that rope. Everything around it, except for the water, froze. What I saw out of the corners of my eyes was as still as a photograph, but the rope and the creek were moving. And then all at once, it was only the rope. The creek held still, and the rope whipped sideways.

I looked away, feeling strange, almost happy. I turned and looked at the wire trashcan, and I felt a little shift, and then the objects of the world—the rope, the beer can, the water—seemed more real, more true, than anything had ever been. And I understood all this in a flash, and then that understanding vanished.

I was still thirsty, and I drank more, finished the can, and the rope hung dead out over the water. I felt warm and queasy, and as I stood, my head felt big. I leaned against the tree, then sat back down, and as though I had a reason to, I sat there and I waited.

I sat there drunk on the creek bank, and my body didn't seem to be a part of me anymore. I looked down at my arms and legs, and they didn't look like mine. I could feel them and move them, but they weren't me. The creek wouldn't stop making its hushing sound. I heard a car coming. It crossed the bridge and went on, until I couldn't hear it anymore. I watched the shadow of the rope, a line of darkness floating on the water.

I held up my hand and looked at it, turned it over and looked at my palm. Everything seemed ridiculous. It all seemed like a joke or, like my mother had said, a mistake.

Why was this hand in the world at all? It didn't have to be, did it? If this hand had never developed—if she'd stopped it right after she got pregnant—the world would have gone on, wouldn't it? The creek would be here. The rope would be here. The shadow.

The bark was rough against my back. Why was the tree there? Why was the creek there? That exact creek and tree and shadow?

My back hurt and my head hurt, and I wanted the world to be different.

3

I stayed there all day, not knowing what I was going to do, until it was almost dark, and I got really thirsty again, and I walked upstream, following a path beside the creek. I'd gone maybe a mile when I came to a clearing and a small house, and there was Albert McGrath, sitting bent over in a straight chair, his elbows on his knees, his hands working. He turned and saw me standing at the path's opening, and he stood up.

I wanted to run, but I remembered what Stroud had said about trying not to hurt his feelings.

I reached into my pocket and took out the little fish I carried with me everywhere, and when he saw it, he limped toward me and took it away, held it up and examined it and gave it back. He walked toward his chair and pointed at the small shapes lying on the ground — two fish and a dog.

He was making that same little half-groan I'd heard him make when he was buying an ice cream at Furlow's.

I said, "Do you have any water?"

He inclined his head to one side. I remembered what everyone had told me — he didn't understand words at all anymore; his brain couldn't make sense of them — but I said it again, louder this time.

"Water? Is there any water?"

He reached into his left pants pocket, took out a knife,

opened it, and handed it toward me. I stepped back, pointed at the house, and walked in that direction. He followed me, knife in hand. When I got to the door, which was standing open, I paused, and he walked inside ahead of me.

I saw that he had a sink, and I went over and turned on the water, let it run cold, then cupped my hands and drank. He stood close behind me as I was drinking, and I wondered if he still held the knife.

He pointed at a loaf of bread and a jar of peanut butter, stood looking at me for a moment, then went over to the sink and washed his hands with hot water and soap and dried them on a paper towel. He took out two slices of bread, spread peanut butter across them, pressed them together, and handed me the sandwich. I ate it quickly, and he made me another one. He opened the refrigerator and took out a can of Dr. Pepper—a drink I had never really liked—and it was cold and good.

He watched me eat, and when I was finished, he walked into the next room and sat on the sofa. The room was bare, except for the couch and two tables, each covered with pieces of wood and piles of shavings and sawdust. He sat there and looked straight ahead, and I did the same. We passed maybe five minutes that way.

He stood up so quickly, I jumped. He hurried into the next room and came back carrying a brown paper bag, sat down again, and reached into the bag and pulled out a photograph and handed it to me—a snapshot of a small brick house with the front door open, a bicycle parked beside the steps, a baseball glove hanging from the handlebars. He leaned over and touched the image of the house and tapped the photo with the tip of his finger. He handed me a close-up of a man with a sleeping baby in his arms. The man wore a red baseball cap propped on the back of his head. He cradled the baby in his left arm, and his right hand seemed to be in motion. Albert McGrath ran a finger across the man, then the baby.

He handed me what looked like a school photograph of a boy. On the back, someone had written *Al, 9th grade.* It looked like a woman's handwriting.

He dumped the photographs onto the table and began to sort through them rapidly, tossing most of them aside. Some fell on the floor. Then he handed me a picture he'd evidently been trying to find—a young woman with long blonde hair and eyes like blue sky at night. I turned it over.

I will love you always. Come home to me. And in a different handwriting at the bottom, *June, 1968.*

He showed me a few more pictures before he started stuffing them back into the bag. When he had put them all away, he crushed the top of the bag into a tight roll and laid it down next to the sofa, and then we just sat there again.

It was dark now, and all around us, waves of steamy sounds rose—cicadas and tree frogs and an owl and the creek hissing against the rocks, and underneath all this, Albert McGrath's soft sound that was almost *oh* but was not, and then I heard it change, and I looked over and saw that he had dozed off. The little groan had gone out of his breathing, which was deeper now, slower. He began to snore—a liquid choking that gurgled and popped and abruptly quit as he struggled for breath until he drew air with a gasping snort. He did this over and over, until his lips began to move, and he made a noise—not his breathing groan, which came out of his throat, but a higher, nasal noise, almost an *h* sound, as if he were trying to say *him* or *hit,* but was unable to get very far.

Those sounds came out of him in bursts I recognized: they were the rhythms of sentences. The nasal *h* sounds rose and fell, and I heard him ask a question, I know I did.

I got up quietly as I could. As I passed through the kitchen, I grabbed a few slices of bread and a can of Dr. Pepper and then eased out the door.

4

I spent the night under the bridge again, stayed there most of the next morning, and then I went back downstream, toward Eva's house, but I didn't know how to get there without going through town. Where the highway forked, the other road turned to the southwest, and so I took it, since Eva lived in that general direction. Whenever I saw a car coming toward me, I ducked into the woods, but after a few cars I realized I looked suspicious doing that, so I ran, head down, along the shoulder of the road. A red pickup with oversized tires slowed down as it passed me, but it didn't stop.

I ran steadily and hard, and I must have covered seven or eight miles when I saw two signs much taller than the surrounding trees, and I knew I was close to an interstate exit. I picked up my pace, and when I came to the overpass, I saw a convenience store and a McDonald's.

I stopped running, walked off into the woods, found a small clearing, and sat down. I had to think about exactly what I was going to do. What if I walked into the store or the McDonald's and they all knew immediately who I was? What if somebody had been there, looking for me? I reached into my shorts pocket for the money I'd stolen from my mother's purse, and I saw for the first time how much it was. I hadn't even looked; I'd just grabbed a few bills, and now I saw that they were hundred dollar bills. Five of them. I sat there for a few minutes, catching my breath and thinking things over, and it occurred to me that five hundred dollars would buy a bus ticket to somewhere pretty far away. Maybe there was a bus stop at the convenience store.

I walked down to the McDonald's and went into the rest room, looked in the mirror, and saw how filthy I was. My face and neck and arms and legs were covered with sweaty grit; my clothes were soppy. I took off my shirt and washed my chest and back and under my arms. I washed my neck and face and my legs, and it wasn't until I'd covered myself with lather and started to rinse off that I noticed there were no paper towels, only a hot-air hand dryer. The toilet paper in the stall was nearly gone. I used what was left to dry myself, but it turned quickly into a crumbling wad that didn't help at all, so I had to use the blow dryer. People kept coming in and out, and I felt silly and embarrassed, drying myself that way. When I got ready to put my shirt back on, I realized that it needed washing too. It was grimy and it stunk, and I could wring the sweat out of it. I washed it and put it back on and went out to the counter, where I ordered a burger and fries and a large drink. When I handed the hundred dollar bill to the girl, she gave me a hard look.

The air conditioning made it too cold for me to stay inside with my wet clothes. I went out and sat at a small table in the play area, where there was a slide and a cage filled with soft rubber balls. A woman at the next table watched a little boy jump around on the balls. My table was slightly behind hers, so I could see them both, and I watched her watch him.

I realized that my mother would be sick by now. She probably didn't know that I had overheard her talking with Stroud, and I hadn't brought anything with me, except the money, so I knew it didn't really look like I had run away. She had a lot of money in her purse, and she might not even miss what I'd taken.

The woman turned and saw me staring at her. "Have you been for a swim?" she asked. My pants and shirt were still soaked, even though they'd dried out a little.

"Yes, ma'am," I said, for some reason. "I mean, no ma'am. I just washed off."

She smiled and nodded and resumed watching the child, who had started throwing the rubber balls against the side of the cage. He'd throw so hard that he'd lose his balance each time, but then he'd do it again. He said, "Watch, Mama." He slung a red ball into the netting, then toppled over sideways.

"That's good, honey," she said. "Don't hurt yourself." She looked back at me and smiled.

She was about my mother's age, maybe a little younger. I wondered where her husband was, or if she had a husband. I wondered if anybody had a normal happy family anymore.

"Do you have a husband?" I asked her, feeling a little shock as I heard the words come out of me.

The woman gave me an amused look. "Why do you ask?"

"I'm sorry," I said. "That's none of my business."

She took a sip on her straw. The drink was empty, the straw gurgled, and she removed the top, tilted the cup back, and now she had a mouth full of ice.

"Do you know if there's a bus station around here anywhere?" I asked her. "I need to catch a bus."

"Nope. Just passing through." She pronounced *through* like *froo*.

"Which way are you headed?" I asked her.

She started chewing the ice, and she nodded and held up one

finger. The ice popped and cracked, and she pointed north and said, "Atlanta."

"I don't guess you could give me a ride up that way," I said. "I know I shouldn't ask."

"That's all right," she said. "You can ask my husband." She pointed to a man who had just walked up.

"Ask me what?"

The woman told him I needed a ride, and the man glared at me, turned and spoke softly to the boy, telling him it was time to go. The boy crawled out of the cage, came around, and took his mother's hand. The man acted like I wasn't even there, and the woman did the same. The little boy waved at me as they walked off. They got into a station wagon and drove away.

I sat there a while longer, then walked over to the convenience store. Three cars were parked outside, and a pickup with Illinois plates was parked at the gas pumps. A bumper sticker on the truck read, "If You Love Something Set It Free. If It Doesn't Come Back To You Hunt It Down And Kill It."

I took off my shoes and washed the mud out of them, using the spigot beside the gas pumps. I removed the laces and pulled out the tongues and set the shoes out to dry in the sun. There was a pay phone outside the store, between a soft-drink machine and what looked like a freezer locker. I crawled up on the freezer, which gave out a constant low buzz, and I leaned back against the wall, which was still hot though it was in the shade now.

And then I heard myself sob. I tried to stop it, but my throat closed off, and I gave out a little whoop and then another sob, just as two boys came out the door—an older boy and another who was about my age. The younger one looked at me and laughed, turned back and said something to the other boy, and they both laughed, heading for the truck with Illinois tags.

I jumped off the freezer, and I shouted, "What did you say?"

Both boys turned and laughed even harder, and I shouted my question again, screamed it at them and called them assholes, and they ran at me and slammed me against the freezer, and it caught me in the back and knocked the wind out of me. The older boy stepped back, the younger one hit me in the mouth and in the nose, and I thought I heard the bone in my nose crack, and blood gushed out all over me.

"Who's the asshole now, asshole?" The boy kicked me in the side and knocked me over, so the blood ran out of my nose onto the dirt and made little clots of bloody mud.

The boys got in their truck and drove off. The store clerk had seen what happened, and he came out and told me the bathroom was around to the side. He said I should wet a paper towel and roll it up under my lip and hold my head back.

I went around to the bathroom, and even with a nose full of blood, I could smell the stink. The toilet was clogged, but that hadn't stopped people from using it. The floor was slick and smeared, the sink crusted black and green, and there was a single paper towel in the dispenser. I pulled it out, dropped it, tried to catch it, and missed. I slid my fingers up into the dispenser and felt around for paper towels that might be stuck inside. Directly in front of me, someone had written in large letters, *Loser,* and I stood staring at the word. The handwriting looked a lot like my own.

I went back and told the man there were no towels in the

bathroom. He reached under the counter and brought out a box of tissues.

"Take these," he said, "and come around here." He led me into a storeroom where there was a large, clean sink and told me to use that. I ran the water as cold as I could get it. I washed my face, and then I folded one of the tissues and pushed it up under my lip. I came back outside, and the man took a good look at my nose.

"Let's see if it's broken." He turned my face left and right, pushed softly at different spots on my nose.

"Got whipped pretty good, didn't you? You ought to see a doctor," he said, "just to make sure it's not broken." He looked outside. "Were you riding with anybody? I didn't see you come up."

"No, sir."

"Well, is there somebody you can call to come get you?"

I told him there might be, and I gave him the name of Eva's mother and asked him to look up the number and dial it for me, if he didn't mind. He dialed and handed me the phone.

When Eva heard my voice, she could barely get her words out. "Where *are* you? Are you all right? Your mother came here looking for you. She's about to go crazy. Are you all right? She was afraid you were dead or kidnapped or something. She's got the sheriff and everybody out hunting for you. Where have you been? Are you all right?"

"I'm all right," I said. "I'm not in any danger. I ran away. But I need you to help me out. Can you do that?"

"You what? What's the matter with you?" She was shouting into the phone now. "You ran away? Are you completely nuts? Are you a total imbecile? Where *are* you?"

"Are you my friend?" I said. "Just tell me that. Are you my friend?"

"Good God."

"Are you?"

"What's the *matter* with you, Lewis? You can't just run away. People have been worried to death."

"Who? Mom? She thinks I'm a mistake."

"You're not making any sense," she said. "Are you crazy?"

"Look," I told her, "I'm coming home, okay?" The words surprised me when I heard them. "But not right now. Tomorrow, for sure, I promise. But right now, I need you to help me out, as a friend."

She didn't say anything, and so I went ahead and told her where I was, and I asked if she knew the place. She still didn't answer. I said I'd been in a fight and I thought my nose might be broken, and my clothes were all wet and I felt sick from swallowing blood, and I asked her if she could find a way to come and get me.

"I really don't want to get involved in this thing, Lewis."

"I'm going back tomorrow. I promise. Nobody will ever have to know you did anything. I won't tell. I'll just walk up to the motel, and it'll all be over. I'll say I've been hiding in the woods for three nights, which will be mostly the truth. But right now, I need some help. When I tell you why I ran away, maybe you'll understand. Please."

"You know, I used to think you were mature for your age, I really did. God." I could hear her laughing unhappily. "That exit where you are is not more than three miles from our house. All you have to do is head east, take a left on the first paved road, then a right onto a dirt road. Follow that for about two miles, and you'll come to the pond and our house. If you make it over here, you can stay a little while, and I'll see how I can help you, but that's the best I can do. You can't stay here overnight; you need to go on back. And how'd you think I could come get you anyway? I can't drive."

"I was thinking of the tractor, I guess."

"Right," she said. "You *are* a child. Just follow the directions I gave you." She hung up without saying goodbye.

But when I'd done what she said, and when I'd finally left the highway and I'd gone a hundred yards along the dirt road, there she was with the tractor. I climbed up beside her, and she turned around and took me to her house. She told me to go in the downstairs bathroom and take a shower and wash off all the blood and dirt. She told me to make sure to wash my hair because there was blood in it.

When I stepped out of the shower, I saw that she had hung some clothes on the inside doorknob — a T-shirt and a pair of men's shorts. The shorts were baggy, and I walked out of the bathroom holding them up, so she got me a belt.

She had heated up some tomato soup, and she'd made me a grilled cheese sandwich. I wasn't really hungry, since I'd eaten so much at McDonald's not long before, but I sat at the table and ate it all.

Afterwards, she made me move over to the sofa and lie down so she could take a look at my nose. It was swollen, a little blue on one side, and I couldn't breathe through it at all.

I told her what had happened — what I'd heard my mother say — and that made a little difference to her, but not much. She said I'd done a stupid and mean and really childish thing, but she said she understood how upset I must have been.

I didn't tell her about Albert McGrath. I started to — I really meant to tell her everything that had happened — but then I didn't. I've never told anybody about him.

She said I could stay out in the boathouse that night, but that I'd have to go back in the morning. They called it a boathouse, but there was no boat. It was just a small cabin full of junk next to the dock. She pointed out a spot where I could sleep, and she brought some quilts and pillows from the house and made a bed on the floor, and that evening, after her mother had come home, she sneaked out with some food. We talked for a while then, but she couldn't stay long. She didn't want her mother to come looking for her.

There was no good place to sit in the boathouse, and we couldn't go out on the dock, and so we both lay down on the quilts. I had my arm around her, but she held herself apart from me, and she was stiff and wouldn't relax. She was never that way before, but I didn't blame her. She told me again that I had no idea what my mother was going through.

We heard thunder far off, and the breeze had picked up, and we heard it moving through the pines. We heard a door slam, a woman's voice calling out, "Evie?," then footsteps.

She jumped up and went out, and I heard her mother ask where she'd been. Eva told her she'd been taking a walk and she'd just wandered into the boathouse. Her mother said something I couldn't make out, and I stood and saw them strolling toward the house.

I woke up and didn't know where I was. Still half asleep, I thought my mother had left the room again, and I stumbled outside. Lightning rippled sideways through the clouds, and thunder shook the trees, and rain came down, and I went back in and lay there fully awake, and the rain started to fall harder on the roof of the boathouse.

And then there she was: not a vision or a dream or even a memory. She came to me as something like knowledge, and I felt it in my arms and legs, in my eyes and my skin and my mouth — my mother had a world inside her, just as I did — and I realized what I had done to her.

The storm went on and on, with high winds and lightning that struck nearby and rain that gusted and beat against the windows all night. If not for that, I would have gone back to the motel right then. I would have let her know I was all right.

5

I woke up with my mother kneeling beside me, her hand on my arm, her face pale and streaked, her hair dirty, and her eyes red. She looked the way she did when she had the flu.

She reached over and pulled me up into her arms, and she hugged me and sobbed and said my name, and then she let me go, raised up and pulled some tissues from her jeans pocket and blew her nose.

I saw Eva and her mother standing in the door of the boathouse. Eva's mother said, "We'll be inside," and they walked off. Eva gave me a strange look.

I told my mother I was sorry for running away. I started to tell her why I'd done it, but she said very softly that she knew what my reason had been, that Eva had told her, and that she was sorry too, that she should never have said what she'd said, but that it didn't matter right now, because my father was dead. He'd had an accident while driving. It had happened last night, not far from Sabbath Creek. She'd called him when they couldn't find me, and he'd been coming to help search for me. He'd been driving too fast, and he'd lost control of the car, and he was dead, and we were going home.

6

Eva's mother had been called to the hospital late that night on a separate emergency, and she'd been there when they brought my father in. She'd recognized the name, and she'd called Eva, who told her I was in the boathouse, and then she'd called the motel and talked to my mother. They had decided to let me sleep until morning before telling me.

We drove back to the motel, and my mother told me to pack my things. She said we'd leave as soon as we could, but first she had to go to the hospital to sign some forms. She gave me the key and let me out in front of the motel and drove off. I watched her go, and it crossed my mind that she might never come back.

I took a shower, put on clean clothes, then walked out behind the motel and along Stroud's driveway. I found him sitting on the patio, smoking a cigarette.

When he saw me, he stood up and stubbed out the cigarette. He said, "Come here, honey," and he stepped over and wrapped his arms around me, and when he let me go, he pulled a chair up close to his, and he sat leaning forward as we talked, his hand on mine.

Nobody else had said it, but Stroud did. "I know you thinking this was your fault."

I knew it was my fault, and he knew it too.

"Yes, sir," I said.

"Look here," he said. "It partly is. That's just the truth. There's no way around it. It partly is, and you'll have to live with that. But you listen to me now. You can't take your daddy's death all on your own shoulders. By yourself. You can't *do that,* even if it is partly your fault. You hear what I'm saying to you?"

I heard a noise behind me. I looked back but didn't see anything except the fence and the trashpile and the old dead oak that rose up behind the trash.

7

We drove home, and my mother followed the interstate as much as possible, but we still had to take some of the same back roads as before. We saw the spot where the old man's collie had died, and we zoomed past Pharaoh's House of Curiosity, still open for business, with its gallon jars of cloudy formaldehyde fixing the ordinary and the bizarre — the little pig with the extra eye that squinted and stared.

And that same night I stood beside my father's body at the funeral home, and I remembered Miss Young saying that Albert McGrath's mother had taken care of him until her death.

I wondered if he'd been there when she died, and if not, how they could have let him know, except by taking him to the body so he could look at it and touch it.

There was a crowd of visitors, but we went in to see my father alone, before anybody else. Mom bent over and kissed his forehead and brushed back his hair, and I stepped up and looked at him, reached down and touched his hand, and he was cold, a cold thing.

I didn't sleep that night. When dawn came, I was still lying on my bed in my old room, where everything was the same but different. My arms and legs felt like they were filled with wet sand. I heard the low buzz of an early lawnmower far off.

My eyes itched and burned, but I didn't rub them. It seemed important not to move.

Within an hour, the house filled with people, most of whom brought food, and all of whom wanted to see me and talk to me and tell me how sorry they were. My friend Andy came over. He usually bulled his way around, trying to make everybody else do what he wanted, but now he was quiet, and we went out and played catch.

And that night, again, I didn't sleep. I lay awake in the dark, and I felt it at last: whatever had been holding on inside of me finally broke—I had no control over my life; I knew it then—and I began to see things.

I saw an old dog tangled in a leash, drowning in a lake.

I saw a man smash his own hand with a crowbar, over and over, then hold out the pulped shape for me to take, a single flower.

I saw the sun blink off and on, off and on, a firefly in a mason jar.

And the next day, the day of the funeral, the world was this way: every word spoken seemed like a joke and a prayer; the edges of things danced and held still; people I'd known all my life seemed like strangers, or like actors playing a part they were not good at, or like animals walking around pretending to be human, odd on their hind legs; and those same people seemed like friends from before this life, as if we'd been together in some earlier world, the glint of their eyes like starlight—those marionettes busy with their own strings, those genuine impostors.

I wanted them to leave me alone, and I wanted them never to leave, and all day I thought about what Stroud had told me.

8

When his boy died in the war, Stroud said, he and Ramona had gone in separate directions. Ramona had stopped going to church, and he had started going every time they held any kind of service.

"Jesus was all I had," he said to me. "That was the only way I made it."

"But Ramona," he said, "she wouldn't listen to nothing about Jesus, not ever again. Here was this good woman that never set out to hurt a soul, the sweetest, most Christian woman anywhere, and who'd never made a big deal out of it, never called attention to herself, just went about doing the Lord's work. She looked out for everybody, young and old, even lowdown trash; she took care of people. And look here: she never said a preaching word in her life, never held herself above anybody else, never let on she'd done the first thing for *any*body."

Stroud sat back and lit a cigarette, and the smoke swirled up and disappeared. His old eyes were red and sad. They had always looked sad, I realized then, even when he was joking with us. They were no different now, except that I felt like, for the first time, I could look back at him. For the first time, somehow, I could look straight at him.

"Little Truman was the one thing Ramona loved in this world. She loved me too, I know that, but I'm just a man. You can replace one man with another one, you can do that. But when your baby's gone, that's the end of something. Ain't nothing coming along to make it better. Not if you tell the truth about it. Time, maybe a little bit. But maybe not even that."

The sky was dark blue, and while he talked, a jet trail grew up from the tree line behind him. The jet, a silver glint, turned toward earth, and the smoky trail looped out behind it.

"So Ramona quit the church, and I went into it all the way, you see. We never did talk about it—wasn't no use—except for that one time. I came back home from church one revival night—they'd had this man from up around Deepstep come in, and he was the kind that wouldn't turn loose of a single soul. He'd look at you one by one, where you sat, and he wasn't about to stop till he saw something in your face. That night, I came home and told Ramona we needed to pray. I tried to put my arms around her, tried to tell her we'd see Truman up in heaven, and she called me a fool. She was standing in the kitchen cutting up a chicken, eleven o'clock at night. That's how she was then—couldn't sit down, always had to be doing something. Cleaning or cooking or washing. She got to where she wouldn't even sleep in the bed some nights. I'd get up in the middle of the night and find her slumped over at the kitchen table, with her face mashed down on the tabletop and her arms hanging down limp at her sides, like somebody had hit her in the head and that's how she fell. She called me a fool and turned with the knife in her hand, chicken blood all over it. 'My boy is as cold as this chicken,' she said. 'He's not in heaven. He's out there at Zion Hill. You know it as well as I do.' She slipped the knife under the chicken's wing and pulled up hard and cut it away, then threw the chicken and the knife down into the sink. She turned and pointed a bloody finger at me and she said, 'Don't you dare preach to me, Truman Stroud. Come in here and want to tell me the *good* news. You listen to me. I've *heard* the *good* news. I know it a whole lot better than you do. Don't you say another word to me about it, not ever. You understand me?'"

Stroud told the story, and the jet trail above the trees gave up its shape. It was a bright day. The whole world seemed clean after the rain.

He said he turned around and went back into the bedroom and prayed, and he went to the revival again the next night. The same preacher was there, just as strong as he'd been the night before, and Stroud stood and witnessed and asked them all for help, asked them all to pray for Ramona.

The people gathered at the front of the church where Stroud was, and they laid their hands on his head while he knelt there, and they said their prayers, and Stroud went home with the song "Precious Lord" almost lifting him off the ground.

"I came in that door right there,"—he pointed at the door that opened into the kitchen—"and I could smell it. She'd been cooking, but I couldn't make out what it was—some kind of meat. Sort of a sweet smell."

She was in the bathtub, her blood cooking in the hot water, cuts from her wrists to her elbow.

"I should have been there with her," he said. "Plain as that, son. I should have been there."

From somewhere far back in the trees there came a burst of noise, a bird's sharp rasp, a single long note, then quiet. Once more, and then it was gone. The old man looked straight into my eyes.

I asked him why God let things like that happen, why God

let my father die in that wreck, and a wasp flew up close to my face, and I pulled away and ducked and swung my hand and slapped at it.

Stroud said, "Be still."

It flew off, then swooped down and came up close to my face again, dipped and feinted and looked like it was going to light on my nose, but swerved backwards, flew between Stroud and me and hung there, and then it turned and sped up and veered out toward the trashpile.

9

August ninth, my fourteenth birthday, we sat in the hot shade, and the preacher said a few words about a man he didn't know. Cars sped by on the highway. A driver leaned on his horn in front of the graveyard.

And far into that night — my eyes wide in the dark, my lips moving on their own — I saw the world go on.

I saw a knife lie down and become a road.

I saw a baby with a face as blank as the head of a match.

I saw a bird dive straight down into deep water without a splash, its feathers stripped away so it became a fish — many rainbows in its new skin, a new heaven in its eyes now.

I saw a skeleton of words, a man of bone, paper stuffed between his jaws. I saw him shuffle and laugh, and grab his black coat, and go.

My father was out there under the ground. I couldn't breathe. I sat up in bed, sucking at the air, ran to the kitchen and bent over the sink and gulped water and stayed there with my head down, dizzy and feverish and then amazed at the bright water swirling into the drain, flashing and breaking beneath my face.

I raised up and looked around me at the empty room. The door to the back porch was open, and I stepped over to close it, and I saw something move.

My mother said, "I'm here, Lewis."

I went out and sat beside her on the love seat, a ruined thing they had dragged onto the porch years ago.

I heard a truck struggle and groan far out on the highway, heard the noise fade and the breeze rise, a rasping in the pines, and I could smell the rain coming on, a hint of metal in the air, and my mother laid her head on my shoulder.

I loved her so much then.

And down the road, a dog began to bark, and a sadness came into his throat, as though he had caught it on the breeze—a whiff of his own life and how far beyond him it was, and would always be.